ELLE GRAY | K.S. GRAY

OLIVIA KNIGHT

FBI MYSTERY THRILLER

BEHIND
CLOSED
DOORS

PROLOGUE

GRAYSON WORTH WAS WAITING FOR THE GOSSIP. THAT was his job, after all. As the stars of the evening walked the red carpet, waving to their fans and posing for pictures in their beautiful dresses that cost more than his yearly salary, Grayson tried not to look desperate as he waved each star over to him with a sickening smile. He was used to butt-kissing at this point, but it was still the least favorite part of his job.

He wanted to catch the big fish of the night, and that meant the stars of *Starless Night,* the clear front-runner for every major award of the evening. Grayson had seen the movie and thought it was fine. The cinematography and performances were good enough, but the plot was hacky and the script was abysmal. In his opinion, it was all the controversies the film had brought to light that had given the movie such a buzz. The affairs, the arguments, the passive aggression... the thought of it sent a shiver down Grayson's spine.

But that was showbiz, wasn't it? The celebrity, the glamour, the dazzling Hollywood lights blinding out everything but the most sensational drama. Who cared about how good a movie was when people could catch up in the tabloids?

He managed to catch the eye of his first victim: Sebastian Morales. He'd been fending off photographers and reporters all evening and had been doing everything in his power to avoid Grayson's gaze, but Grayson had a way of luring people in. He swore he saw a sigh escape Sebastian as he walked over, adjusting the jacket of a designer suit that clearly cost upwards of ten thousand dollars. *Must be nice,* Grayson thought.

"Hey there, Sebastian. Thanks for joining me tonight!" Grayson said, widening his grin until his face hurt.

"Sure, good to be here," Sebastian muttered with zero conviction. *Someone won't be winning the Best Actor award tonight...*

"May I ask what you're wearing tonight, for your fans?"

Sebastian pursed his lips, looking down at the black-and-green floral-patterned jacket as if he'd just picked it out of a dumpster. "Oh, I couldn't tell you. My stylist deals with all of that. Something expensive, no doubt."

Grayson smiled. On one hand, dealing with guys like Sebastian was tedious, but on the other, it made it easy to be rude about them later in his column. At least that way, he didn't have to feel guilty about spilling the tea.

"Well, I'm skirting around what people really want to know anyway. Let's hear it from the horse's mouth... what's really going on between you and Landon Brown? I hear there was some pretty vicious fighting on set..."

Sebastian's cheeks turned red, and Grayson smirked to himself. He knew there was more going on between the two actors than some petty fight on set, but he didn't need to say that out loud. It was one of the few secrets he was willing to keep.

"There's always talk from the media when a new movie comes out," Sebastian said, his jaw clenched. "They spin stories about what the actors do and talk about on set."

"But there was undeniable tension, right? I mean, from what the director, Frank Fisher, has described…"

"Are we here to talk about on-set drama or about my work?" Sebastian asked coldly. Grayson smiled.

"Both, darling. Always both. But a simple 'no comment' will suffice…"

"No comment," Sebastian muttered, looking away from Grayson. Both of them knew that those two simple words spoke louder than any others anyway.

Sebastian turned on a dime, plastered on a grin for the cameras, and walked off without another word. Grayson couldn't blame him. He worked in a cutthroat business. Unnerving men like Sebastian was part of the job. But he had to admit, the rumors surrounding the production of *Starless Night* had him more curious than most. So little had been said in the public eye, and yet everyone knew something strange was going on during that movie. The public hungered for it, and Grayson was determined to feed them.

It wasn't long until Grayson hooked his next catch of the day. She looked glamorous as ever, but underneath the expertly-applied makeup, Miranda Morgan had bags under her beautiful blue eyes. As she drifted over to speak with him, Grayson offered her a sympathetic look, to which she averted her gaze.

"Miranda… you look absolutely stunning tonight. Is that a Romano design I see you wearing?"

Miranda smoothed down the cream silk of her dress. It was simple yet stunning. Miranda never needed to try to look like the most beautiful woman on the red carpet. "Good eye, Grayson. It's good to speak with you again."

Grayson knew that was a lie, but he and Miranda had become well acquainted, especially in recent years. Not that it made them friends, but Grayson did feel a twinge of concern for her. She must be exhausted, given all the drama in her life at that moment.

"I have to ask... the questions on everybody's minds. You worked on *Starless Night* while also going to court with the star—your husband, Landon Brown. You're divorcing him, isn't that right?"

"It's not a secret," Miranda said, her soft blue eyes filled with a pain that seemed to have made its home permanently inside her.

"No, that much is true. The secret is *why*, isn't it? The world is desperate to know... what caused one of the A-list power couples of Hollywood to end their relationship? And how did it feel to work alongside the man who has caused you so much pain?"

"I would suggest that you don't put words in my mouth," Miranda said, fiddling with one of her golden curls. "Whatever pain I might be experiencing is mine to keep. I don't owe the public an insight into it. All anybody needs to know is that Landon and I are no longer compatible. I might even go as far as to say we never were. Divorces happen all the time. And we move on. Now, I can tell you more about *Starless Night,* if you're interested?"

"Of course, I'm interested," Grayson lied. He suppressed a sigh as Miranda began to rattle off all of the same old stories she'd clearly told every reporter in the city. *Well played, Miranda. Well played.*

The main event had yet to arrive. Grayson, and every other person there, every red-carpet reporter, every photographer, every screaming fan, every anxious actor, director, and starlet, was waiting for Landon Brown to show up. Because really, it didn't matter who was there if he wasn't. He was the person everyone in Hollywood couldn't resist loving or loathing. Some said he was the most honest, most down-to-earth man they'd ever met. Others said he was an unstoppable narcissist, a plague on Hollywood, a man who should never be allowed out in the public eye. Grayson had met him and done business with him enough to know that both sides could be true. Either opinion was suited to Landon, and Grayson was sure that was deliberate. That's what made him so fascinating—a flawed man with talent and sex appeal oozing out of him.

He was born to be a star.

And the moment he showed up, everything changed.

Landon Brown stepped out of a slick black car to the cheers of the hundreds of fans lining the red carpet. Every head turned to face him. He was grinning like he truly understood that he owned each and every person there. Like he knew they'd all been waiting for him this entire time. His entire life. As the fans screamed his name, he strutted onto the carpet, a slight swagger in his step. Grayson narrowed his eyes.

The man was drunk. No, not drunk—he was absolutely wasted.

Grayson smirked to himself. Now there was a story. Any other reporter might be subtle enough not to comment on the man's alcohol issues, knowing it would lose favor with his fans. Ever since his stint in rehab and his much publicized comeback, he'd been stone-cold sober, and his fans were so proud of him, flooding social media with messages of support and love.

No one wanted to say a bad word against Landon Brown— not even his estranged wife, staring back at him from ahead on the red carpet, her lips tightly pressed together. Not even Sebastian Morales or Frank Fisher, who by all rumors had vicious things to say to his face on set. But they'd never tell the press. They'd dance around the subject, but never talk.

But Grayson Worth would. It was what he did best.

The reporters seemed to close in like a swarm as Landon made his way down the red carpet. He seemed to be taking his time, blowing kisses to the crowd, ignoring every person he passed. His eyes were glazed over, but nobody would be able to tell. It would be a wonder if he could see any of them at all. Grayson stepped forward, right into Landon's eye line. He knew Landon would stop for him, as he always did. He had to. They had a deal. A deal that benefited both parties, but mostly Grayson. Those were his favorite kinds of deals.

"Landon!" he cried cheerily, waving at him like they were old friends, even though their relationship was far from friendship. "Come here, let's talk about that suit you're wearing…"

Landon's eyes fell on Grayson for the briefest of moments. It was then that Grayson noticed just how far gone Landon looked to be. His beautiful face was marred with dark circles, his eyes lifeless and bloodshot. His cheeks seemed hollow. To the naked eye, he was still ethereal, untouchable, perfect. But Grayson knew better. Something was wrong.

"Landon!" he said again, but this time, it was almost like voicing a question... as if he wasn't really sure it was him at all.

Landon's eyes slid from him slowly, like it was an effort to drag his eyes away. And then his smile returned, the type of smile that the audience was waiting for. The show must always go on...

And Landon walked right past Grayson.

Grayson could barely believe what had happened. He wasn't used to being left in the dust like this. They had a deal. It wasn't supposed to go like this. Grayson clenched his jaw.

He would make sure that Landon regretted that later.

It wasn't long before everyone headed inside for the awards ceremony. Grayson tended to be alone at these kinds of events, and it was less awkward with a drink in his hand. He headed to the bar while he waited for everything to kick off. Landon was due on the stage to emcee the entire evening, which Grayson scoffed at inside his head. *Good luck presenting the show when you're clearly drunk or high as a kite. Or both.*

He drank heavily from his margarita and ordered another before he reached the bottom of his glass. He had some catching up to do if he was going to match Landon's level. But it was only by the time he reached the end of his third margarita that he realized that the show was supposed to have begun already. He checked his watch. It was due to begin at eight. Now, it was several minutes past.

Where the hell was Landon?

Landon Brown came to slowly, his vision blurring before his eyes. Pain blossomed across his face like a deadly flower. *What the hell happened?* He tried to blink away the pain, but it only made his vision worse. So, he gritted his teeth and waited for the world to stop spinning.

It took him a few moments to realize that his teeth were sinking into a gag. He squirmed, trying to cry out, but the gag muffled him, and his body was tightly secured by rope. He looked around himself desperately, wondering where he'd been taken.

Before his eyes was a TV screen. It was the broadcast of the awards event. Someone was standing up on the stage, where he was supposed to be. Anger coursed through him. *This was meant to be* my *gig,* he thought, fury bubbling inside him. Some unknown actor was standing in his spot, holding the envelopes, stealing his moment of glory.

"And the winner of Best Actress is..." the man said, opening the envelope. But as he read the card within, he fell silent. He clamped a hand to his mouth and the audience began to murmur. Landon struggled against his bindings. What was going on? He was missing everything...

"Um... this isn't right," the actor finally said, looking around for someone to assist him. Landon smirked, despite himself. Did someone unfavorable win? If his ex-wife had taken the award despite her terrible performance in *Starless Night,* that would be a terrible shock.

"Um... it says... it says 'Landon Brown will never be seen again.'"

Landon's blood ran cold. And it was only then that he realized what terrible danger he was in. Hazy memories came back to him, and now he was piecing together what had happened. He strained his mind to remember. He had been in the dressing room, about to start...

"Five minutes, Landon," called out the stage manager as she bustled quickly past his door. He immediately turned away and tried to hide the flask he was taking a swig from. He couldn't have people spreading rumors... not now.

He looked up in the mirror and splashed a little water on his face. The makeup crew would complain, but they could fix it over the commercials. They always had something to complain about.

While he toweled off, he heard footsteps enter his room behind him and close the door. Probably just some production assistant reminding him of the time. Again.

"*What is it now?*" *he grumbled, but the person didn't respond. He finally placed the towel down and turned around to find the intruder staring intently at him. Too intently.*

"*Can I help you?*" *he finally asked.*

Again, there was no response for a long moment. Landon scoffed and turned back to the mirror, closing his eyes and rubbing his temples with two fingers. A headache was coming on, but as long as he kept himself at enough of a buzz, it would be fine. He'd hoped to have one last swig before going on, but this intruder was putting a cramp in his plans.

"*Don't you remember your promise?*" *the intruder finally asked.*

He opened his eyes now, staring forward at his reflection to find the intruder much closer to him, a storm like fury and heartbreak in their eyes.

"*What the hell are you talking about?*" *he asked.*

But the answer never came.

He opened his mouth to call out to the stage manager, to his agent, to someone, *but before he could he felt a sharp, sudden pain in his back. Like a needle sting. And not even a minute later, everything went black.*

He was a captive. He was going to suffer for what he'd done, for how he'd treated people. He was finally about to get a comeuppance. He fought harder now against his bindings, but there was no budging them. He was stuck. And soon, he would be taken away to face some awful fate…

"Don't worry," his captor's voice suddenly interrupted his thoughts. "You and I are going to have a wonderful time together."

CHAPTER ONE

L IFE HAD SLOWED DOWN A LITTLE FOR OLIVIA KNIGHT. IT was a Sunday morning in late January when she woke to the sun streaming in through the window and the smell of breakfast wafting in from the other room. She smiled. It seemed like Brock had decided to cook her something to start off her day.

She put on her robe and headed toward the kitchen. Brock was unpacking a big brown bag, and Olivia rolled her eyes with a smile.

"Should have known better than to think you'd cooked," she said.

Brock winked. "Where would you ever get that idea from? Why would I cook when I can get breakfast from the diner?"

"I swear, you're going to end up forking over your entire life savings to that place," Olivia said, reaching on her tiptoes to kiss Brock's cheek.

"Money well spent," he cracked with his signature grin. He seemed to get more handsome every day, a thought that would have once made her cringe. But for once, she was happy. Everything was good. She didn't need to push away her positive thoughts.

"Do you want to eat on the sofa in our pajamas and watch that book adaptation you've been raving about?"

Olivia smiled. "You read my mind."

"Well, I figured I'd have to get it over and done with at some point... what is it again? Another one of your period dramas?"

"It's Jane Eyre. Surely, you've heard of Jane Eyre?"

Brock shrugged, stealing a piece of bacon as he unpacked their breakfast. "I don't really vibe with historical fiction. But if you like it, then I'll try to like it. That's the deal, isn't it?"

He's perfect, Olivia thought to herself. Then she really did cringe at herself. She helped Brock plate up their food, and then they retreated to the sofa to watch Olivia's show. It was a peaceful retreat, sitting there quietly and enjoying the morning. Not so long ago, she would've likely spent her Sunday mornings working for lack of something better to do, and with a borderline obsession too. Now, she let the workaholic within her rest, and she felt better for it.

After they finished an episode of the show, Brock took Olivia's plate for her, and she stayed curled up on the sofa, feeling content. It was only when Brock spoke again that he burst her bubble.

"What time is your mom coming over?"

Olivia sighed. "Midday, I think."

"Try to sound more excited."

"It's not that I don't want to see her," Olivia protested. "It's just that she loves Belle Grove a little too much. She starts using words like 'quaint' and 'cozy' every time she mentions it. She always wants to do a full tour of the place, as if there are more than three things to see and do."

"I thought that's why you liked it here? Because it's quiet and calm... because nothing much changes in an ever-changing world."

"That's exactly why I like it. But I don't need to walk through the forest again to show Mom the sights, and I really don't need to hear her talk about the architecture again. Belle Grove stays the same, and so do our conversations."

Brock tsked. "You know, she's trying hard. Harder than ever. That's why she does it. She's trying to reconnect with you."

Olivia sighed. He was right. Even though Jean had apologized a thousand times for her disappearance, for shattering Olivia's life into pieces, there were still moments when it felt like they were both walking on eggshells. Christmas had been so perfect between them, when they talked and enjoyed each other's company just like in the old days. But since then, it felt like there had been an awkwardness between them. Like they'd moved too hard and too fast toward their past. Olivia didn't feel angry toward her anymore, but sometimes, she wondered if things could ever go back to the way they once were.

"She doesn't need to try so hard. I'm not expecting miracles."

Brock barked out a laugh. "This is Jean Knight we're talking about here. Asking her to not try hard is… well, it's like asking *you* to not try hard."

Olivia chuckled, forcing herself off the sofa. "Well, I guess I'd better get ready for the day then. I still haven't figured out what to do for dinner."

"I have. I'm going to cook."

Olivia scoffed. "You're going to cook? You literally just got our breakfast from the diner."

"I know. I didn't want to overdo it, cooking twice in one day," Brock said with a sly wink. "I'll make steak. I know she likes it, and I can cook a good one. Maybe some roasted veggies too? I'll take care of the kitchen, and you can both catch up while I cook."

Olivia's heart swelled with warmth. Her mother clearly wasn't the only one going out of her way to make an effort. It made her so happy knowing that Brock wanted to impress her family. It was certainly a step up from even her ex-fiancé Tom.

"That… that would be very nice. Thank you, Brock."

The grin returned. "Don't worry about a thing. We've got all the ingredients. I'll take care of it."

"If you give us food poisoning, I won't be happy."

"Yes, ma'am."

It was just shy of midday when Jean arrived at the house. Olivia took a deep breath before she opened the door, fixing a smile on her face. She wanted her mom to feel welcome, to know that despite her earlier conversation with Brock, she was more than glad to see her.

"Hello, darling!" Jean said, sweeping into the house with a kiss on Olivia's cheek. She thrust a bottle of red wine into her hand.

Olivia looked down at the bottle of merlot. "Hey, Mom… oh, wow, this is very formal."

Olivia knew she didn't imagine the blush on her mother's cheeks. "Oh, this old thing? I pulled it out of storage. Figured we could put it to better use than lying around back home! It's meant to go very well with steak, which I believe Brock is cooking us for dinner?"

Olivia glanced back at Brock, who was lounging on the sofa with a sheepish grin.

"We text a little," he admitted with a shrug. Olivia shook her head at him. He was doing so much to be a part of her life. How could she ever fault him again when he was doing everything he could to make her life better?

"Did you hear about that man on the news?" Jean asked, making herself comfortable on the sofa beside Brock. Olivia sat down on the opposite chair, amused by the newfound friendship between her partner and her mother.

"You might have to be a bit more specific, Mom."

"The actor, Landon Brown! The one that played Mr. Rochester in the new Jane Eyre adaptation."

"Oh, him," Olivia said, surprised that she'd seen it. Maybe she'd been studying up on Olivia's favorite things to make for good conversation. The thought made Olivia feel a little uneasy. When did her mom, such a headstrong and independent woman, become such a people pleaser?

"What's happened to him?" Brock asked. Jean turned to him, her expression bordering on excitement.

"Well, that's the question! He seems to have disappeared. No one really knows what's going on. He was supposed to emcee an awards show two days ago, but after walking the red carpet, he just disappeared. And then there was a suspicious note swapped into one of the results envelopes; it claimed that Landon would never be seen again."

"Now that is juicy," Brock said, looking amused. "I mean, presumably this is some kind of stunt? I've heard things about him. He's known for his flair. He always seems to be up to something. So, did he just do some kind of disappearing act? It's probably to promote that new movie he's in. Starlight something?"

"*Starless Night*," Jean supplied. "And that seems to be the big theory. But it's interesting, isn't it? You'd think if it were a stunt he'd be front and center, not completely gone."

Olivia shrugged. "I don't know why people get so invested in celebrities' comings and goings. I mean, I get it to some extent. The glitz, the glamour... people like to imagine what it's like to be among the stars and live their lives. But the obsession with where they go and what they do...you're probably right. It's likely a stunt. I feel like these big Hollywood stars and productions are getting more creative. No one has the attention span to simply sit down and watch a movie trailer anymore. It's all ten-second videos on social media and big public productions. Like the promotion for that film, *Screamers*... did you see all those paid actors, standing at football games with their hands on their faces, reenacting that creepy painting? It was all to draw attention to some low-budget horror movie. I guess it worked, though, since people were talking about it."

Brock smirked. "For someone not interested in pop culture, you sure seem to know a lot about it."

Olivia blushed. "Alright, I guess I may get sucked in now and again. But I stand by what I said. I couldn't care less about the ridiculous things famous people do. All that time and money on their hands, and they just go around making trouble for everyone else to clean up. No doubt the police are going to get roped in if he doesn't show up soon. And then what happens? Public time and money get spent on keeping up with the lives of the elite."

"You're no fun," Brock said. "If it's a stunt, I think it's cool. Well, depending on how it ends. As long as he doesn't cause too much trouble, I don't see the harm in it."

"When have cheap pranks ever ended well?" Olivia countered.

"You watch. This will end terribly."

"Bring on the chaos," Jean said with a smile. "I can't help thinking that you're wrong about celebrity culture. It gives some escapism from real life, doesn't it? The way you lose yourself in a book, others lose themselves in the lives of the rich and famous. Because just like stories, nothing you see in Hollywood is real. It's all manufactured. Mark my words ... if this is all some promotional tactic, the media will spin it as this great story. The man probably just left through the back door and retreated to some secret vacation home in another country. He'll show up again in a few weeks and get everyone talking about him, just like we are now. And when it happens, we'll all be glued to our screens, wanting to know what happened."

Olivia snorted. "Speak for yourself. I think I'll pass. The only stories I want to hear on the news are about world affairs."

"I bet you're fun at parties," Jean said. Olivia laughed despite herself, shaking her head. As they all shared in laughter, she forgot about the strangeness between her and her mother. She spent a pleasant afternoon talking to Brock and Jean, debating topics and swapping stories. By the time they all sat down for dinner later that evening, everything seemed to be back to how it should be.

"This is delicious," Jean complimented Brock as she sliced her steak into small bite-sized pieces. "The peppercorn sauce is incredible!"

"I made it myself," Brock said with a sly glance in Olivia's direction. They both knew he'd rushed out last minute to find a jar because he'd forgotten to pick up some heavy cream the day before.

"It's nice not to cook for once," Olivia said pointedly, though she didn't really mind. When she cooked, she wasn't responsible for doing the dishes.

"Well, it *does* mean you're on dish duty tonight," Brock said, reading her mind.

"Listen to the pair of you! Like an old married couple!" Jean said with a laugh. She glanced at her daughter. "It won't be long before wedding bells are chiming."

And just like that, the good mood of the day disappeared. Olivia and Brock glanced at one another awkwardly before averting their gazes. This wasn't something that Olivia expected to come up at dinner. They were still taking things slowly between them, enjoying one another's company. The time that they'd known each other had been so chaotic that the last thing they needed was added pressure. Marriage was the last thing either of them wanted to think about.

And now the comment was hanging in the air like an elephant in the room.

Olivia was relieved to hear her work phone ringing on the other side of the room. Taking a deep breath, she stood from her chair, trying not to look anyone in the eye.

"I have to get that," she murmured, walking away with two pairs of eyes staring at her back. When she saw Jonathan's name on her phone, she picked up quickly.

"Got something for you Knight. Hope I'm not interrupting your Sunday."

"No, not at all," Olivia said, glad to hear his voice. "What's going on?"

"I have a new case for you and Tanner. I suppose you've heard about the disappearance of Landon Brown?"

Olivia frowned. "Really? They're bringing the FBI in on this?"

"We can't dismiss this as something not serious, Knight. No one has seen him or heard from him since the awards ceremony, and the LAPD has forwarded this to us for help. If he isn't found soon, there will be an uproar. And given his high profile, it's important that he's found."

"I see," Olivia said carefully. She didn't see how Landon Brown was more important than any other person, but she knew Jonathan was right. If he wasn't found, the media would have a field day soon enough.

"I'm entrusting this case to you two for another reason. I want to keep your involvement in this case on the down-low. That means going undercover—fishing around for information. The kinds of people you'll need to mingle with won't take too well to having the FBI in their business. Do you understand?"

"I do," Olivia said. She knew Hollywood wasn't as glitzy as it often seemed. It was a breeding ground for drugs, crime, and all sorts of reckless behavior. Celebrities believed they were untouchable. If they caught wind that they were being investigated, Olivia and Brock would never find out anything.

"So, you understand the need for discretion. Which is where Tanner comes in. He has a contact in Hollywood who will be able to get you into some exclusive events without it seeming suspicious."

"He does?" Olivia said, blinking several times. It was the first she'd heard of it.

"Yes. His ex-girlfriend, Yara Montague. Have you heard of her?"

Olivia's mouth dropped open. "Of course, I have. She played Elizabeth in the *Pride and Prejudice* remake…" It was another show she'd forced Brock to watch. How had he not mentioned his ex being on their screen at the time?

"You do love a costume drama, don't you?" Jonathan remarked, sounding amused. "Well, anyway, she will be very helpful to the case I believe. I'll brief her shortly on what we'll need from her, but in the meantime, you and Brock need to get down here so we can talk more before I ship you out to Hollywood. Can you come now? I'd like you on that plane tonight."

"Yes, that shouldn't be an issue," Olivia said, thinking about the awkward silence she'd left behind at the dinner table. She was more than happy to find a lucky escape.

"Excellent. I'll see you soon."

Olivia hung up the call and returned to the table. Brock and Jean still seemed to be feeling the discomfort in the air because they both looked up eagerly at her return.

"Well, looks like we're going to be the first to figure out what happened to Landon Brown after all," Olivia said. "We've been assigned his case. I'm sorry, Mom, but we have to go."

"Of course. I understand entirely," Jean said with a relieved smile, as if she was looking for a way out too. "Call me?"

"I will this week."

Jean left with a brief kiss on Olivia's cheek and headed out to her car. Brock's shoulders seemed to sag in relief as he turned back to Olivia.

"Well, shall we?"

Olivia raised an eyebrow. "Yes, we shall." She paused. "And on the way there, maybe you can tell me about Yara Montague."

CHAPTER
TWO

"**O**LIVIA, I'M SORRY I DIDN'T TELL YOU ABOUT YARA. I didn't think it was a good idea."

Olivia was looking out the window as they drove up to Washington. It had been a quiet drive so far with the aftermath of dinner hanging over their heads. There was a lot to talk about, but Olivia didn't really feel like talking about it. Still, she knew it was going to sour their evening if they didn't, so she carefully edged around the subject.

"I'm sure you had good intentions. You always do. But I've said it before, and I'll say it again... you know everything about me. You have since the beginning. I know I'm an open book, and you're always fighting to keep your pages closed, but I thought we'd moved past that."

"We *have*. Look, Yara was a childhood sweetheart of mine. We're talking a six-month fling when we were in high school. It was never that serious. We stayed friends afterward, which just goes to show how little it meant to us both. And then she went on to be this big Hollywood star, and now I only hear from her a few times a year, which suits us both just fine. It's been maybe three years since I saw her in person."

"So why couldn't you tell me this before?"

Brock sighed, drumming his fingers on the steering wheel. "It's like you said before; people act differently when it comes to celebrities. I guess I figured that because she's famous, you might view her differently from one of my other exes. And I didn't want to casually bring it up while we were watching one of your favorite shows. I'd never ruin *Pride and Prejudice* for you like that."

Olivia's lips quirked into a small smile. He knew her so well. And she totally understood his reasoning now.

He reached over to touch Olivia's thigh. "After we watched the show, there just wasn't a good opportunity to bring it up again, and I never imagined it would matter. I didn't think it was likely to ever come into play, but I guess I was wrong. I'm sorry if it upset you."

She returned his gaze. "It didn't upset me. Not in the way you think. I just wish I had known. I know I let my emotions get the better of me sometimes, but I'm not as fragile as you might think. I just wish you would tell me about this kind of stuff."

"And I will. In fact, I'll tell you everything now. Yara was my first kiss as a kid. We were maybe fifteen then, before we actually took an interest in each other. And I was so bad at kissing that I accidentally bit her lip and she ran home with blood trailing down her chin."

Olivia laughed. "You? Brock the heartthrob, a bad kisser?"

Brock quirked his eyebrow. "You think I'm a heartthrob?"

She shoved his arm. "Don't fish for compliments. It's unbecoming."

"You should know by now never to present me with an opportunity to have my ego fed. It's constantly hungry."

Olivia chuckled, looking out the window again. She felt a little better now, even though she was anxious about meeting Yara and working with her.

But what bothered her more now was the comment her mother had made about marriage. It was a joke, she knew that much, but it had hit a sensitive spot. Olivia had already had one unsuccessful engagement, and she didn't like to think about having another. Especially not with Brock, when he meant so much to her. More than anyone ever had before. Her stomach twisted. She and Brock hadn't even gotten around to talking about their future yet. Olivia had imagined it plenty of times, but those fantasies stayed firmly locked away in her mind. She didn't want to put pressure on this thing they had going between them and risk losing it all. She wanted, more than anything, for things to be simple, whatever that meant for them. She'd had a lifetime of complications.

And what she shared with Brock hadn't always been easy, but it felt easy now. Even when they had disagreements or squabbles, she never felt deep-rooted anxiety about it. She felt safe in the position they'd taken up with one another.

That was until her mom opened her mouth.

Olivia held back a sigh. She hoped that Brock might forget the conversation and they could pretend like it hadn't happened, at least for a while. They had a new case to focus on, and the last thing Olivia needed was to be distracted by domestic affairs.

Her phone buzzed in her pocket, and she knew who it would be before she checked it.

Mom: *Did I make things awkward? I'm sorry, darling.*

Olivia tucked her phone back into her pocket. She wasn't ready to answer. She wasn't angry with her but maybe a little frustrated. She just needed time to recover from the shock of it. It was typical that just when she was beginning to feel normal around her family again, something would throw a monkey wrench in the works. Olivia told herself that the moment the case was over, she would revisit her thoughts and talk things over with her mom.

They arrived in DC, and Olivia sat up a little straighter and prepared herself for the briefing. She had to admit, the case was starting to interest her. She wasn't sure it could be deemed an important case if Landon had simply run off for some peace and quiet, but clearly something had happened for the LAPD to immediately request the Bureau's assistance. She felt a twinge of pride in her chest, knowing she and Brock had been trusted to handle it. It was always nice when someone had faith in her.

Brock parked, and Olivia followed him to Jonathan's office. She felt a little excitement bubbling inside her. Having some time off had been nice, but now, she was ready to get started again with something juicy. She hoped the case wouldn't turn out to be a huge waste of time.

Jonathan looked more relaxed than he usually did when they entered his office. He was slumped a little in his chair with no sign of his usually rigid posture. She supposed this was about as close as they could ever get to seeing him relax on a weekend. He gestured for them to sit down.

"Have a seat. I just got off the phone with Yara Montague. She said she's looking forward to seeing you, Brock, and to meeting your partner."

"Well, let's just hope this trip out to Hollywood is worth our time. Who wants to spend a week going to fancy parties and hanging out with celebrities?" Brock said with a grin. "Apart from Olivia, of course."

Olivia rolled her eyes. "I like fancy parties. I just would rather attend one in good company."

"It's lucky you're going with me then, isn't it?" Brock said with a smirk.

"Alright, enough of this. I still want you to take this case very seriously. I know all signs are pointing to this being some kind of practical joke on Mr. Brown's part, but there are some reasons to actually be concerned."

"Which are?" Olivia asked.

"We can't ignore the fact that a threat was made against him in the envelope presented at the awards show. If it wasn't Landon who planted it, then someone very smart set this whole thing up. You see, there's only a seven-minute window in which he could've disappeared. A stage manager called to him five minutes before he was due to go on stage, and he was then seen hanging around, waiting for his cue. But after that, there wasn't a single sighting of him. So, either he made a very quick getaway, or someone managed to get him out of the building, past a bunch of security, without being seen."

"It's definitely impressive, whichever way you look at it. I heard there was more security that night than at any other awards ceremony."

"It doesn't surprise me," Jonathan said. "According to my contacts, Landon Brown was not a popular choice to host the awards. He's become a sort of controversial figure in Hollywood. He was evidently intoxicated on the red carpet, despite a very public recent stint in rehab and an insistence that he's been sober. The set of his latest movie, *Starless Night*, was by all accounts a disaster. He had a nasty falling out with the director and another costar. And to top it all off, he and his wife, another costar, began divorce proceedings during filming."

Brock whistled. "Sounds like a busy man."

"Seems so. It's all tied up with his history and reputation as well: allegations that he cheated on his wife multiple times, gambling and drinking to excess. He's been arrested several times for drunken charges—as I mentioned, he went to rehab and was primed for a big public comeback and new squeaky-clean image, but it seems it just didn't take. To put it plainly, the man is a nightmare. But still, the public loves him."

"Of course, they do. He's a handsome, reckless white man in Hollywood. What's not to love?" Olivia said sarcastically. Jonathan raised an eyebrow.

"I take it you're not impressed by the likes of Landon Brown?"

"He can act; I'll give him that. But he holds far too much power in his hands. I think he knows it too. If this is in fact a ploy for publicity, then wasting our time is going to be his downfall."

"Then that's even more reason to take this seriously. I want you to find him and figure out what happened that night at the awards ceremony. That's where Yara comes in. You'll fly out tonight to meet her, and then she's going to take you to some very exclusive events. There, you will be mingling with some of the biggest names in the business, including every single person that Landon has a rivalry with. I want you to play the field, find out what they're all talking about. But I want you to be subtle. They can't know that you're with the FBI, or the whole operation will fall apart. Put out feelers, but don't push too hard. Let's see what we can find out before we go in all guns blazing. If they feel they're in safe company, their lips will be pretty loose. Let them believe they're untouchable."

"What about *actual* work?" Olivia pushed. "Have we checked for fingerprints on the envelope that contained the threat against Landon? Have we checked all of the footage from the venue, interviewed everyone who was there? And if we're working on the assumption that this isn't some game of Landon's, then shouldn't we consider the profile of our kidnapper? Did they really pull off this operation alone? Was there someone to handle Landon and another person to switch the envelopes?"

"All good questions, Olivia, and I assure you, I'm not ignoring them. The LAPD is handling those things and other tasks. But for now, I need the two of you to focus on the brief I've given you. You're both young and attractive. You're the perfect candidates for this specific part of the operation; you'll blend right in at the parties. Once you've dug a little deeper, I'll tell you what to do next."

"You hear that, Olivia? That's the sound of yet another person feeding my ego," Brock said with a grin. He turned back to Jonathan. "We're ready for anything."

"Good. Flight leaves in an hour. I believe Yara has taken on the task of fitting a wardrobe for you both for the occasion. You'll need to look the part to attend the events, which means expensive threads."

"I'm liking this case more and more," Brock grinned, standing up. "Let's go party."

CHAPTER
THREE

L ANDING IN LA FELT LIKE A DREAM TO OLIVIA. THERE WAS a glorious sunset lighting up the sky, and she knew that in a few hours, she would be attending a swanky party in a beautiful dress, her partner and best friend on her arm. Sure, she wasn't into celebrities and their culture, but she would never say no to playing dress up and spending an evening with Brock.

Still, she had to remind herself that there was important business to attend to. She couldn't let her guard down, and she had to be hyperaware of her surroundings. She was looking for someone to slip up and give away more than they should. She didn't think it would be too difficult to find someone with loose lips among the drunk elite, but then again, she had never been to a party like this before. She couldn't truly know what to expect, and that meant staying on her toes.

And first, she had to meet Brock's ex. Her stomach twisted as they got into the hired car that had been sent to pick them up from the airport. She trusted Brock when he'd told her that Yara was a thing of the past. That wasn't the issue, really. It just intimidated her a little to go up against someone whose life was so drastically different from her own. Yara was rich and talented and wildly successful. Olivia had never been rich, though she had to count herself as talented, too, just in a different way. She was also successful, but being an FBI agent seemed so perfunctory next to the life of a bona fide movie star. She and Yara were so unlike one another that it made her nervous to compare herself and feel small.

Brock reached for her hand as they drove through the streets of LA. "Stop worrying," he told her with a gentle smile. "You're going to love Yara. And she's going to *adore* you."

Olivia smiled back, trying to push aside her nerves. She knew that there would be no competition between them because neither of them wanted to outdo the other. Yara didn't want what Olivia now had, and Olivia didn't crave the life that Yara led. She took a deep breath and reminded herself that they were simply two women who loved and appreciated Brock, which meant they had something in common.

The car took them up into the Hollywood hills, and Olivia couldn't help marveling at the houses around her. She could see the appeal of being rich and famous, if only to live in such a gorgeous place. But Olivia knew that celebrity life was rarely as glamorous as it seemed, and given the nature of the case they were working, she certainly didn't want to go chasing the spotlight. It was never the life she'd intended to live, and a few fancy houses wouldn't change her opinion on that. She had everything she wanted and needed back in Belle Grove.

When they reached Yara Montague's property and passed through the metal gates, Olivia tried not to stare at the grandeur of the house. It was three stories tall and as wide as three ordinary houses. Three black, shiny sports cars were parked out front, as if on display for the whole world to see. Yara Montague was rich, and she was letting the world know it.

"Thank you," Olivia said to the driver as she stepped out of the car onto shaky legs. She had been expecting something spectacular, but this was something else. Brock didn't seem too fazed by it all, and Olivia wondered if he'd visited Yara here before. She didn't feel the need to ask though. Brock wasn't really a materialistic guy. She could see how a big house like this would be far from what he wanted. Back when he'd worked for his grandfather, he'd been offered a glimpse into how life could be if he chose the path of riches and glory. He'd turned it down then, and Olivia saw no reason why it would interest him now.

And when Yara stepped out of her front doors, wearing a silk robe and a pearly white smile, Olivia's nerves loosened a little. She ran across the driveway in her slippers and threw her arms around Brock for a hug. He laughed a little, hugging her back, but he was smiling at Olivia over his shoulder.

"It's been far too long," she said in a pleasant voice, which sounded like a mash-up between an American and British accent. Olivia supposed that working on British period dramas had done that to her.

Yara stepped away from Brock and turned her attention to Olivia with a delighted squeal. She rushed forward and cupped Olivia's cheeks in her hands, smiling radiantly at her.

"My *God*, you're gorgeous," she told Olivia, as if she herself weren't a six-foot-tall goddess with a model's figure and perfect porcelain skin. She barely looked real to Olivia with her effortless chestnut curls falling on her shoulders and blue eyes staring at her intently. It made Olivia laugh a little.

"Thank you."

"You should be on a screen," Yara declared dramatically. "You're simply too lovely to be an FBI agent. You and Brock both."

"I should have mentioned that Yara is a little… enthusiastic," Brock teased, digging his hands into his pocket. Yara waved him off.

"It would be worrying if I wasn't. I am an actress, after all. Please, come inside. I have a gorgeous bottle of Dom Perignon just waiting to be opened."

"You know we're here to work, Yara."

"You're *here* to blend into the Hollywood scene," Yara corrected him with a teasing wink. "And that means being a little tipsy at all times. Come, come. You have a lot to catch up on if you're going to be successful with this case."

Olivia couldn't help feeling like she had collided with a hurricane as Yara took her arm and pulled her toward the house. It seemed impossible to take in the moment when there was so much going on around her. She felt better after Yara had whisked them through the stunning hallway filled with modern art, to the living room, which was a space much too large for the two sofas and modern white fireplace. The walls were white, too, sparsely decorated with art. It made the room feel even bigger, but Olivia felt it was better than having so much stuff crowding in on them— especially when Yara's presence was already making her feel a little claustrophobic, despite her pleasantness.

A bucket of ice sat on the table between the sofas, and a bottle of rosé was perfectly perched on top. Yara popped the cork with the ease of someone who was used to casually dining on five-hundred-dollar wines. She expertly poured out three glasses and then handed them out, practically buzzing with excitement. She raised the glass to them both.

"Cheers to working together," she said with a wide smile. Olivia tried to smile back, still a little overwhelmed by everything.

"Cheers," she repeated. She hadn't planned to drink what she was offered, but she found herself raising the glass to her mouth and sampling the cool, crisp wine. It was good. Very good. It sent a little shiver down her spine, and Yara laughed at her pleasantly.

"Good, right? I have at least one glass a day. They say it's good for your complexion. Helps the circulation in your face."

Olivia wasn't shocked by the comment. It seemed to be the crux of celebrity life. They had everything they could possibly want, and why shouldn't they? Of course, they'd come up with some reason to keep up appearances and lavishly spend. Olivia took one look at Yara's sparkling smile and knew that she'd never faced hardship once in her life. That should be a good thing, and yet it only made her feel more uncomfortable about the way that celebrity culture worked. The taste of the bubbly turned sour in her mouth.

"Unfortunately, Yara, we're not really here to enjoy ourselves," Brock said, bringing Olivia back to the room. She was glad he had been the one to say it. She didn't want to be rude when Yara was trying to welcome them so nicely. But she seemed unfazed, simply sinking into the sofa with an elongated sigh.

"Oh, Brock. You were always supposed to be the fun one!"

"I'll bet you don't drink on the job either, Yara."

Yara's lips twisted into a smile. "Think again."

"Yara..."

"Fine, fine," she relented, waving him off. "Sit down. Tell me what I can do to help." Olivia and Brock sat down opposite Yara on the leather sofas. Olivia was sure they looked out of place in their scruffy traveling clothes. Brock cleared his throat.

"We need to know everything you can tell us about Landon Brown. We need to know about his connections, who he liked and disliked, who liked or disliked him... we need the truth—not whatever spin his PR team puts on things. It might help us figure out what led to his disappearance."

"Well, I can certainly help with that," Yara said with a lofty smile. It occurred to Olivia that Yara was almost a caricature, so over the top that it was hard to take her seriously at all. *The whole world's a stage,* Olivia thought to herself. She wondered if everyone she'd come across would be playing a part the way Yara was.

"Where to start..." Yara said thoughtfully. "Well, I guess it's important to note that Landon Brown is a very unusual man. I would describe him as being an enigma. I don't believe that anyone truly knows him. For years, he and Miranda seemed so untouchable. Every time he would get in trouble, every time he'd party, every time he'd get caught, it would just be swept under the rug."

"Until he started getting arrested," Olivia said.

Yara shrugged. "It happens. Once it got out in front of the cameras, it was kind of over. That's why he set up this whole rehab stint. People love a good comeback story."

"Was it all for show, though?" Brock asked. "Or was it real?"

Yara giggled. "Brock, babe. It's Hollywood. Everything's for show."

"If he was drinking that much on the red carpet, he probably relapsed a while ago," Olivia pointed out. "Has he been ... partying again? Being erratic lately?"

Yara leaned forward with a conspiratorial expression on her face. "I think Miranda was going to go public with the fact that he hadn't really gone sober—use it as leverage for the divorce, which was really tilting away from her favor."

Brock and Olivia traded glances at that. "So, she'd have motive to get him out of the way," Olivia noted.

"Life would certainly be simpler for him if he just disappeared," Yara said simply. "And now, by the looks of it, he has. Either she's breathing a sigh of relief, or she's the one behind it. Miranda is a smart woman. I'd think that she's entirely capable of making a man disappear."

"In the middle of her divorce proceedings? Don't you think that's a little risky?"

"Of course, it's risky. So is making a person disappear in the middle of a huge event. Someone pulled it off somehow, so why not her? I do think it's a possibility."

Olivia took another sip of her champagne. She was curious about Landon's ex. She was another actress that Olivia had seen on her screens many times, and it was hard for her to imagine her as cold and calculating. Miranda was the sort of actress who'd been typecast, always playing the softer characters in movies. Olivia had to remind herself that it didn't mean she knew anything about who this woman was in real life.

"What about the set of *Starless Night*?" Brock asked. "I heard there were some pretty significant difficulties there. Did you hear anything?"

She shrugged. "Nothing more than what you'd know. I've never worked with Landon, but I've heard he's a nightmare on set. Especially when he's been drinking. I've heard stories. Always making outlandish demands, staying in his trailer to get wasted. Constantly fighting with his costars. But he can get away with it."

"What did the director think of that?"

"He chose Landon for the role hoping he'd stay clean. I don't know if he knew Landon was still drinking, and maybe he had regrets about it. This was a passion project for him, and Landon nearly ruined it. Burned bridges with both him and Sebastian. He's aged ten years since the start of filming. Looks terrible."

"Maybe he should drink some of this rosé to get some circulation in his face," Olivia remarked.

If Yara picked up on the sarcasm, she didn't say it. "Right? Everyone could use some pampering."

"You think he hates Landon for it?"

"He would have every right to. But then again... Landon doesn't really have friends in our circles. You'll see tonight. I don't think anyone is upset that he's gone, really. Not even Miranda. He's always been trouble. In some ways, if he really is gone... I think some people will be breathing a sigh of relief."

"And who do you think is capable of making him disappear?" Brock asked.

Yara laughed. "Any one of them. This place is cutthroat, Brock. You'd be shocked by these people if you knew them—if you *really* knew them. Some of them like to create drama just to keep things interesting."

The comment made Olivia uneasy. The whole environment in Hollywood seemed toxic to her. How could no one care that a man had gone missing? Even if it was some prank that Landon was running, did it really not matter to anyone? Was it all just a game to them?

"What time can we get to this party? I'm eager to hear what people are saying," Brock asked, checking his watch. Yara tutted.

"Sweet, innocent Brock. You're far too early. The party tonight won't truly begin until midnight. That's the way we do things here."

"Midnight?" Brock frowned. "I was hoping to be in bed by then..."

"This is LA. Nobody goes to bed until the early hours of the morning. Besides, I'll need time to get you both ready for the party. You can't go as you are. We're talking brand new clothes— designer, of course. Allow me to be your fairy godmother for the night. And then, let me show you how to party like a Hollywood star."

CHAPTER
FOUR

66 **A**RE YOU NEARLY READY, OLIVIA? I WANT TO SEE your dress!"

Olivia was standing in one of Yara's many bathrooms, looking at herself in a full-length mirror. She could barely believe that Yara had managed to find her a dress on such short notice, and she couldn't believe how different she looked. Yara had hired a makeup artist and hair stylist for them, and they'd sat in her dressing room being pampered while Yara talked nonstop. Now, an hour and a half later, she was looking elegant and refined in an emerald green dress made of silk, her hair tousled and her eyes shimmering with a subtle green shadow. She felt a little nervous as she examined herself. With Brock waiting for her outside, she didn't have long to savor the moment, but it felt good to get dressed up. She couldn't wait to see Brock's reaction.

"I'm coming out now," she replied, heading for the door. She had to admit it would be nice to see Brock in a suit too. He could pull off anything he wore, but no doubt he would look dapper in an expensive designer suit.

The pair of them locked eyes on one another as Olivia emerged from the bathroom. Olivia was right. Brock looked more handsome than ever in a cobalt blue suit, perfectly matched to the dress she was wearing. She watched his eyes roam over her body, a slow smile forming on his lips.

"You don't need me to tell you how good you look… but I'm going to anyway," he said with a grin. "Yara picked the perfect dress for you."

Olivia blushed. "Thank you. She did a good job with you too."

Brock grabbed Olivia by her waist and pulled her in close to him. "We'll be the best dressed couple at the party."

"I doubt that. There will be people there wearing designs worth double our collective net worth."

"But are any of them as gorgeous as you? No, I don't think so," Brock murmured, planting a kiss just below her ear. Olivia shivered a little. She still didn't really know how to take a compliment, but that had never stopped Brock from showering them on her. For some reason, what her mom had said about them getting married flicked through her mind, and suddenly, the possibility didn't seem so outlandish.

Olivia cleared her throat and moved away from Brock, her cheeks burning. It was like she was anxious that he might hear her thoughts and know how deep into this thing she truly was. She walked over to the dresser to smooth her hair and check that her cheeks weren't as red as they felt.

Brock seemed to be unfazed by her moment of nervousness. He threw himself down on the bed, watching Olivia get ready as he lay on his back.

"Nice of Yara to offer to host us for tonight, wasn't it? Are you okay with staying here?"

"Of course, I am. She's… nice."

Brock laughed. "You can say she's crazy. No one would disagree. But I meant... you know. You were worried about her before."

"Oh, please. I wasn't worried about her."

Brock smirked. "No?"

Olivia rolled her eyes, holding back a smile. "No. Not worried at all. What about your multi-millionaire, beautiful, movie star ex would have me worried?"

"You're such a terrible liar."

Olivia turned to Brock. "And you're the most faithful man I've ever known. So no, I'm not worried—not about you and not about her. If she wants you... well, tough. She can't have you."

"That's fighting talk."

"Well, I'm a fighter," Olivia said plainly, fixing her hair one last time in the mirror. And it was true. There was a blaze in her eyes. She was ready for the evening. Ready to do her job, but also ready to push any doubts she had out of sight and out of mind. She and Brock were a team. They had survived much more than some ex-girlfriend from years ago.

"That you are," Brock said. "That's why I love you."

Olivia turned to him with a smile that she couldn't hold back. "I love you too. Are we ready to do this?"

"Absolutely. But first, let me get a photo of you. I want to remember forever just how incredible you look tonight."

Forever. As Olivia posed for a photograph for Brock, that word replayed in her mind over and over. Did he mean that? It wasn't the kind of word she would just throw around. What did it mean to him?

She wanted to believe that forever was a possibility for them. But it was still so early in their relationship, and Olivia knew better than most how the world could suddenly come crashing down around a person. It had happened to her more times than she could count. And she was scared that if she wanted it too much, if she pushed this thing between them too hard, that she might somehow lose it forever.

But she didn't want to think about that now. She couldn't afford to if she was going to get her head in the game for the party.

It was just after eleven o'clock, and Brock took her arm to lead her downstairs to meet with Yara. They still had a little time, but they had to be well-prepared for what they were getting into.

Yara was waiting for them in the living room. She clapped her hands in delight at the sight of them, matching as a pair together. She herself was wearing a silver gown that was almost sheer, showing off the skin beneath her dress. Olivia almost didn't know where to look with such a skimpy outfit on her new acquaintance.

"You two look *adorable* together. I should be a stylist," Yara declared. "Are you ready to party?"

"We have some ground rules to go over first," Brock said pointedly. "We need to decide what our story is."

"Easy," Yara said smoothly. "You're my childhood best friend, and you're in LA because your girlfriend, Olivia, is looking to make it as an actress. I promised to show you both the ropes and give you an insight into Hollywood life."

"How generous of you," Brock said with a roll of his eyes and a small smile. "Okay, that works. Are you sure you're going to be able to get us into this venue? Isn't there like a guest list or something?"

Yara tsked. "It's not a venue; it's a house. We're going to Mollie Minter's house. Her parties are legendary, and anyone who is anyone will be there. I guarantee Sebastian Morales will be there—and Frank Fisher. Miranda might not show; she's been a little reclusive since the divorce... but then again, she will have the sense to know it'll look weird if she's not around. I think she'll be there."

"Good. We'll need to speak to all of them at some point. But tonight is about putting out feelers. No one should know who we are or what we're doing," Brock said. "If you hear anything, Yara, anything of interest..."

"You'll be the first to know," Yara replied with a smug smile. "I'm not one to withhold gossip."

"Alright. Then I guess we're ready to do this," Olivia said. There were butterflies in her stomach. This was a new kind of case for her, and she wanted to reach out and grab the opportunities in front of her.

"I've got a driver waiting for us out front," Yara said. "He'll pick us up somewhere around five. You think you guys can last that long?"

Brock and Olivia exchanged a pained glance, at which Yara laughed out loud.

"You guys are so sweet," she teased as they headed out to the car. "The car will be out in front of the house whenever you want to leave. The driver can always come back for me."

"Thanks, Yara. Though I definitely think we're going to need a late night if we want to gather some real information," Olivia said.

It was quite the treat to drive through the Hollywood Hills in the middle of the night. Olivia had visited the city a few times before, but only briefly. When it was lit up, the whole place seemed to sparkle with opportunity and life. Olivia might not be a fan of the Hollywood lifestyle, but she could imagine how visiting as a tourist would be fun. There was a sheen of magic coating the place, making it seem so utterly perfect. But Olivia was sure that what lay beneath that facade was something much darker and more sinister. Perhaps she'd catch a glimpse of the real side of Hollywood tonight.

When they pulled up to their destination, Olivia was horrified to see how many people were already there. The driveway to the house was packed with sleek black cars similar to the one they were in, and celebrities were milling around outside, laughing, drinking, smoking. It was clear that everyone within a two-mile radius was crammed into the party, and considering how loud the party was, it was a good thing. Olivia wouldn't want to be the host's neighbor that night, especially not without an exclusive invite.

"I thought you said no one arrives until midnight?" Brock asked, sounding mildly horrified. Yara tutted.

"No one with any class does. It's called being fashionably late. You see all these C-listers getting wasted? They're social climbers. They pad the party outside so when the likes of us arrive, there's someone around to admire us as we enter the building."

Olivia snorted out a laugh, but Yara clearly wasn't joking because she didn't return the laugh. Olivia suddenly felt wary of the woman. How self-centered could a person be?

And if everyone was looking their way, it would ruin their plans. The hope was to blend in, not to be noticed. Yara looked back from the passenger seat and smiled.

"Don't worry. No one here is going to think anything of your presence. They're all too drunk to see faces, let alone remember them. You can slip right in to the party and do what you need to do. But act a little drunk if you can. No one here stays sober long."

"Thanks, Yara," Brock said as the driver parked and they all got out of the car. "I owe you one for this."

"Maybe when this is over, we can go on a real night out. Just like old times," Yara said with an enigmatic smile. "Sometimes I miss the simplicity of just going to some gross, old club and dancing the night away."

"That would be nice," Brock said in a non-convincing voice. Olivia knew that Brock's clubbing days were well behind him too.

Yara motioned for them to follow her, and Olivia wobbled across the gravel toward the house. She was already regretting wearing heels. But for the sake of blending in, she powered through, trying to look like she belonged.

Inside the house, she was shocked to find that it smelled of cigarette smoke and weed. Olivia had never thought she'd see people smoking inside at a posh celebrity party, but the scent wafted past her and made her nostrils itch. Yara greeted people cheerily as they weaved through the crowds, but Olivia couldn't see many faces through the haze of smoke in the air. She resisted the urge to cough as bassy music filled her ears. This hadn't been what she expected at all. The house was beautiful, filled with art and high ceilings just like Yara's home, but the people inside it seemed to have made the place drop in value. Yara was right: these people were here to get famous, to get noticed. They were like seat fillers—the sort of guests you invited to a wedding or a party to make up the numbers. The real stars were elsewhere, she supposed. She would have bet anything they liked to keep a barrier between themselves and what they considered to be the riffraff.

"Let's go to the bar!" Yara said as they continued on through the house. Olivia was expecting some kind of self-serve bar with bottles of drinks available freely, but then they entered a huge room where the music seemed to be coming from, and she realized that they were in a sort of club. There was a proper bar with several bartenders making cocktails, handing out glasses of champagne and pulling pints. Olivia couldn't imagine having enough money to build a quasi-club inside her house, but she did think it was one of the more fun uses of a person's money.

The problem was that she could barely hear a thing. She exchanged a glance with Brock. How were they supposed to eavesdrop and gather information if they couldn't hear anything?

Yara, seemingly picking up on Olivia's concern, put her mouth close to her ear to speak to her.

"You won't catch the A-listers in here," she shouted to be heard. "We'll head to the conservatory next. It's quieter… and the people in there are the kind you'll want to speak with."

Olivia nodded to let her know she understood. She just needed to be more patient. Despite her better judgment, she found herself wanting to have a drink in her hand. She had no plans to be drunk and out of hand, but she did think it would be best to have something to drink, especially if she wanted to blend into the crowd. Everyone around her was intoxicated, dancing wildly, and bumping into them as they weaved to the bar.

And that's when Olivia spotted Miranda Morgan.

She hadn't been expecting to see one of the most famous, most respected actresses in Hollywood like this, eyes closed and hair loose as she danced wildly. She was clearly drunk, or high, or both. *So she showed up after all,* Olivia thought to herself. She didn't look like someone who was concerned that her ex-husband had gone missing. In fact, she looked oddly free.

And that was a red flag right off the bat.

"Do you see what I see?" Olivia said into Brock's ear. He nodded, turning back to her.

"She's blitzed," Brock said. "She must be, to be acting so casual. Doesn't she know that everyone is watching her?"

"Maybe that's exactly it," Olivia murmured. "She knows she's being watched. And she's prepared for it."

CHAPTER
FIVE

IT DIDN'T TAKE LONG TO ADJUST TO HOW LOUD THE PARTY was. Olivia soon realized that she could hear well enough if she concentrated, so she and Brock danced a little in the crowded bar while listening for snippets of conversation.

Two women standing close by were shouting to one another about the disappearance of Landon Brown. Olivia caught Brock's eye, and he nodded to affirm that he was listening too. The two women were clearly too drunk to care who heard them.

"What do you think? Do you think he just ran off somewhere?"

"I hear he's got a *private island*. The man is *filthy rich*."

"I heard that too. Apparently fifty models are living on the island, and they just wait for him to show up so that they can be there for him."

Olivia rolled her eyes. She could believe that Landon owned a private island, considering how rich and famous he was, but the notion that he kept women trapped there for his own entertainment was much too far-fetched in her mind.

"What I wouldn't give to belong to Landon Brown," one of them gushed.

"What if it isn't true? What if he's ... what if he's *dead?*"

"He can't be dead. He's too rich to die."

Olivia spluttered at the drunken comment. She'd officially heard enough. Yara had disappeared into the party, and Olivia hoped she might be getting farther with the investigation than she and Brock were. It was almost one o'clock, and all they'd heard so far was ridiculous rumors and drunken ramblings.

"I think we need to get out of here," Olivia shouted into Brock's ear. "We need to be around the kind of people who actually knew Landon... not the people spreading gossip about him."

"You're right," Brock said. "But where do we even start?"

"I think we're just going to have to explore until we start seeing familiar faces. That's when we'll know we're on the right track. Yara said something about a conservatory... let's find that. Presumably it'll be at the back of the house, by the garden."

"Okay. I'll follow your lead."

They pushed through the crowd. The loud music was really starting to give Olivia a headache, but she wasn't about to give up and go home. Her champagne was still half full in her hand, and she'd been nursing it slowly for the past hour. It might be enough to keep her going.

As they walked through the crowd, Olivia spotted a familiar figure retreating from the dance floor. It was Miranda, drunker than ever and heading for the bathroom that bordered the bar. Olivia's heart leapt in her chest. Perhaps this would be a good opportunity to get a sense of her. Olivia nudged Brock.

"Go on without me," she said in his ear. "I just saw Miranda heading toward the bathroom. I'll see if I can talk to her, or at least listen to her conversations."

"Okay. I'll take a look around the house and see what I can find. Be careful."

Brock kissed her lightly before heading into the crowd. The sensation lingered on her lips like champagne bubbles as she headed to the bathroom. His kiss was a welcome feeling in such an unfamiliar place. She hoped it would give her the confidence to seem like she belonged at this strange party.

The bathroom was huge, and didn't seem like a bathroom in a home at all. There were five stalls and as many sinks. The room was made entirely of marble, and it was light and airy after the suffocation of the dance floor. There weren't many people in there, just a group of girls giggling at the sinks as they snorted lines, and a woman being violently sick in one of the stalls. Olivia's heart sank. She knew the woman had to be Miranda.

"She's a mess," one of the women sadly whispered as Miranda retched loudly in the stall.

"You would be, too, if Landon Brown divorced you," another of the women hissed. "But still. Kind of pathetic, the way she's acting."

Olivia swept past the women and headed into the stall next to Miranda's. She shut the door and waited in there for a moment, pretending to use the bathroom. She heard the other women leave in a flurry of laughter, and only then did she flush the toilet and head out to the sinks to wash her hands.

In the mirror, she caught sight of Miranda. She was on her knees in front of the toilet, not even bothering to shut the door. Her dress was hiked up a little, and her cheek was pressed to the toilet seat, a little drool coming from her lips as she stared vacantly into space. Olivia's heart seized. She didn't look like she was in a good way.

"Excuse me, ma'am?" Olivia said gently. "Is everything okay?"

Miranda moaned in response. Olivia was beginning to grow concerned that she might be in some serious trouble. She finished washing her hands and then, before she could stop herself, she headed into Miranda's stall and shut the door behind her.

Miranda barely moved as she saw Olivia entering. Olivia grabbed her a little tissue and wiped the vomit from her lips. Even in such a state, Miranda was stunningly beautiful. Her blue eyes were sparkling with unshed tears, and her lips were plump, like she'd just been kissed. Her blonde curls were dipping inside the toilet bowl, but Olivia gently moved them back behind her shoulders. The last thing Miranda needed was to return to the party with vomit in her hair.

"Thank you…" Miranda murmured. "What's your name?"

"I'm Olivia."

"I haven't seen you before… are you new in town?"

"That's right. I'm here with Yara Montague. She's a friend of mine helping me break in the industry."

"Huh…Yara… that's nice."

Miranda clearly didn't have the energy to say much else. Olivia floundered for something to say to her.

"Can I get you anything? Some water, maybe? It might make you feel better."

"No, no… I just want to curl up here and die," Miranda murmured. "You're new to Hollywood so I guess you won't know this… but life isn't as glamorous as it might seem."

Olivia didn't seem to think any of it was glamorous so far, especially not when Miranda had her head halfway down the toilet, but she didn't say that out loud. To her horror, Miranda sniffed, and tears began to fall down her cheeks, her perfect porcelain skin shining with the teardrops.

"I thought I was going to live a fairytale," she whispered. "I thought that once I left Ohio behind, I would live in a fantasy. That's what I was promised when I came to Hollywood. They don't tell you how easily dreams become nightmares, do they?"

Olivia said nothing. She had a feeling that Miranda, like many other actors, was good at monologuing. She let out a long, mournful sigh, leaning her head against the toilet seat again.

"I wanted so badly for my life to be perfect. Everyone thought it was. I married the most eligible man on earth… except he's not eligible at all. I married a goddamn monster."

Olivia held her breath. She was worried that saying anything now would stop Miranda from speaking so freely. She had her eyes closed. It was like she had forgotten Olivia was even there, and that was fine by her. If it kept her talking, then it didn't matter.

"My husband... so handsome, so charming, so enigmatic," Miranda mumbled. "Everyone tells me that. Everyone tells me how lucky I was to hold him for even a short time. Like he's something so unattainable, so precious that no one can hold him down. Well, there was a time when people said that about me. I came to this city with nothing... but all it takes is to be beautiful if you want to succeed. And back then, every man wanted me. Half the women too. But I wanted *him*. And I got him. I thought I was so special for that. Everybody did."

She sniffled and Olivia handed her another square of toilet paper. "I thought we would rule the world. But nobody talks about how hard marriage is. How you have to pretend it doesn't bother you when your husband sleeps with half of Hollywood. How you have to pretend it doesn't hurt when he makes *promises* he never intends to keep. When you're treated as an extension of him instead of your own person. And now look at me. Sad and coked up and crying in a bathroom because my stupid ex-husband ruined everything."

Olivia didn't say a word. There was something so disturbing about Miranda's speech. Like she was still dancing around some topic, like she was still covering Landon's back. Olivia desperately wanted to know what she was hiding and why.

Miranda's head lolled to the side, off the seat, and Olivia was quick to catch her and stop her from smacking her head. Miranda let out a sad laugh, returning to her previous position sloped over the toilet.

"I could've been so much more than this," she murmured. "If only I wasn't a fool in love."

"I'm sorry," Olivia offered lamely.

Her eyes snapped open and met Olivia's. She suddenly seemed angry, her eyes clear and hardened. "Landon ruined my life, you know. And I've protected him for so long... but why shouldn't everyone know what he did to me? Why shouldn't everyone know that the divorce was on *my* terms, not his? He wanted me to keep covering for him, to act as his shield against the world. Women hated me because they couldn't have him. Men hated me because I didn't choose them. I became his shield—his battering ram for getting through his life unscathed. But not anymore. I deserve better. He should be the one lying in a bathroom, *mourning* the life he lost through this marriage. I would've given him everything. But he had the nerve… the *nerve* to hit me."

"He hit you?" Olivia blurted out. She knew she was there to be a sounding board, not to comment, but she was shocked by the admission. Some part of her felt it wasn't possible. Some part of her felt like she knew the people she'd seen on the screen, like an acquaintance that was a friend of a friend. The kind of person you heard gossip about, enough to build them up in your mind as a solid person and personality. Would Landon, the hero of every movie, the heartthrob of America, truly hit his wife?

"He's got you all wrapped around his little finger," Miranda spat bitterly, like she was reading Olivia's mind. "*Perfect Landon.* Look at his nice comeback. Incapable of hurting a fly. Well, I was the fly, and he smacked me so hard that I thought I'd never recover. All because I called him out on his drinking and cheating. He made *promises*, you know. Real promises. He said he'd fix everything. And he almost did. And before I knew it, he became the same old Landon… I'd had enough. And I told him I would leave him. So, he slapped me. And right then… right then I knew he never loved me. How can… how can anybody hurt the one they love that way?" Miranda was close to tears again. "How could he hurt me that way?"

Olivia wanted to hug Miranda close. She was too intoxicated to be weaving such lies. She was speaking from the heart to the first person who was willing to listen to her. Olivia got the sense that Miranda Morgan had been alone for a very long time. She reached out and took her hand. Miranda sniffed.

"I don't usually drink," she sobbed. "Because Landon was always the drunk between us. Someone had to make sure he got home safe when he'd drank half the bar and smoked all the weed in LA. And it made him so much of a monster that I never wanted to be that way. But tonight… with him gone… I couldn't be sober. I needed to let go."

"I understand."

Olivia wasn't sure that Miranda even really heard her. Her hand was limp in Olivia's, like she couldn't feel her touch on her skin. Miranda sat up a little, wobbling like a bobblehead in a car.

"I shouldn't have come here," Miranda whispered. "People will be talking about me … what must they think? They must think I have so much to gain with Landon gone. What if they think I did this? Especially… especially after what I did for revenge …"

Olivia's heart skipped a beat. What did she mean by revenge? Was Miranda really about to confess something terrible she'd done?

But when Miranda moaned dramatically, Olivia got the sense that she was dealing with something else. Something a little more trivial than making a man disappear.

"Sleeping with Frank was a mistake," she muttered. "But it was the only way I could think of to hurt him. After so long with Landon, trying so hard to please him… I wanted a man to worship the ground I walk on. And Frank did that. It was bonus points for me because Landon hates Frank so much. He always complained how much Frank asked of him on set… like that's not his *job*. But that makes me look even worse. Sleeping with the enemy… I look guilty. But I'm not. Even after everything, I could never hurt Landon. My curse is that I'll love him until the end of my days… and just like everyone else, he won't love me back."

With that, Miranda threw her head forward and vomited into the toilet while Olivia quickly grabbed her hair and held it back. Olivia was sure that Miranda wouldn't recall any of the conversation they'd had the next day, and it was likely for the best. For now, at least, Olivia's cover wasn't blown, but she'd learned a lot. She decided she would find Miranda's driver and get her sent home. The poor woman needed a good night's sleep, not a party.

Besides, Olivia wanted to tell Brock about what she'd found out. And to learn more about the strange world she'd stepped into.

CHAPTER SIX

I T TOOK A WHILE FOR OLIVIA TO GET MIRANDA OUT TO HER car and find her driver, and in that time, she drew more attention than she would've liked. Olivia could feel eyes boring into the back of her head, hear people whispering about who she was and why she was there. She didn't want people to notice her presence there, worried it would blow her cover, but there was no way she was leaving Miranda alone and vulnerable in the bathroom. She'd be better off at home where she could at least sleep off her hangover in peace and not embarrass herself any further. Olivia at least owed her that after the insight she had offered Olivia into her life with Landon.

Olivia couldn't imagine how difficult it had been for Miranda in recent years. A divorce was never easy, but it was near impossible for a woman like her who was under scrutiny from the public eye, who was the least favorite half of a celebrity couple, who was harboring a secret about Hollywood's best-loved man. Not only was he clearly an alcoholic, but he was a womanizer and an abuser. And Miranda had been carrying the burden of all of that alone, keeping her head down. She had clearly kept the abuse she'd suffered a secret—and with good reason. Miranda clearly understood what it would mean for her to stand up against Landon. More hatred from the public. Being accused of being a liar. Losing work opportunities, friends, connections. It was a tale as old as time—a powerful woman going up against a significantly more powerful man never ended well.

And the world would never know how Miranda had suffered.

Olivia could hear people talking about her as she wove back through the crowds to try to find Brock. There were whispers about her behavior that night. Some deemed it inappropriate when her ex-husband was missing. Others thought she was trying to act normally to cover the tracks of what she'd done. It seemed that plenty of people were willing to hold her responsible for his disappearance.

But Olivia had knowledge that none of them had, and it made her almost certain that Miranda wasn't behind it all. Drunk truths had spilled from her mouth to a stranger because she was lonely, because she had no one else to turn to. She clearly thought Olivia was some nobody who would never sell her out. And she was right, in some ways. Olivia wouldn't tell anyone about the abuse except Brock. Not even Yara could know. She'd been told that information in confidence, and she swore to herself to only use that information to solve the case.

It took Olivia quite a while to weave through the house and find Brock. She passed through corridors where familiar faces were dotted around, talking to one another. Seeing people she recognized from TV but didn't know was a strange sensation. Rooms were full of strangers who seemed so familiar to her. It was like having déjà vu.

The feeling waned when she finally found Brock in what she presumed was the conservatory. It was a huge add-on to the back of the house made entirely out of glass. It had started to rain outside, and the sound of water pitter-pattering on the roof was calming after the ordeal with Miranda.

Brock was standing to one side, talking to Yara in a low voice. Their faces were close together, and Olivia blushed, feeling like she had entered into a private moment. She had to take a second to compose herself, to remind herself that Yara was simply an ex from his past who probably thought nothing about being up close and personal with him. In the few hours she'd known Yara, she had been similarly close to her, and it meant nothing at all. Olivia took a breath.

She approached them, and Yara ushered her over with a genuine smile. It made Olivia fully relax once again.

"Join the huddle," Yara said with a conspiratorial giggle. "We're catching up about what we've discovered."

"Here?" Olivia asked, glancing around. The atmosphere was quieter here, and she was worried about being overheard. As much as she wanted to spill the information about what she'd discovered, she didn't want to blow their cover. She suspected they weren't the only ones at the party attempting to eavesdrop.

"I was just telling Yara to calm down a little," Brock said, raising an eyebrow at Yara's giggles. "I think she's had a few too many."

"Alright, party pooper," she said with a giggle. "But I'll behave, I swear. Let me do the rounds again. I'll only report back if I find something juicy."

Yara left with a cheery wave to someone across the room. Brock chuckled fondly at her retreating figure.

"She's one of a kind, that woman," Brock said. Then he leaned in and brushed his lips against Olivia's cheeks. "I've missed you out here. You were gone for a long time."

"Getting soppy, are we? Has someone else had a few too many drinks?" Olivia murmured in his ear. He chuckled again.

"I might have had a couple. But I'm staying sharp, I promise. I take it your trip to the bathroom was a success?"

"Brock, that sounds so gross. But yes, it was… in a way. I spoke to Miranda."

"You did?" Brock said, dropping his voice to a whisper. "And?"

"And… she told me some pretty crazy stuff. She was absolutely wasted. Crying, breaking down. She was in really bad shape. I just got her driver to take her home. She said her marriage to Landon was loveless, that he was out of control… not only did he cheat on her, but he also hit her."

Brock's eyes softened. "That's terrible."

"She said that's the real reason for their divorce. Or one of them. It sounds like he's made her life pretty miserable. But I don't believe she had anything to do with his disappearance."

"Why not?"

"You saw how she was earlier… she was in no shape to lie. I think that much alcohol usually acts as a truth serum. She said she never wished him any harm, even after everything he did to her. I think she just wanted a simple life. And now that he's gone…"

"It complicates things for her," Brock finished. "Because people will start pointing fingers in her direction."

"Exactly. She has very little to gain from this. I think her reputation will take a hit the longer Landon is missing. She knows that too. But there was one thing she did admit to me… something that might be linked to Landon."

Brock raised an eyebrow expectantly. Olivia looked around to make sure they weren't being overheard, but they were standing far from anyone else in the conservatory, and everyone was engrossed in their own conversations. Olivia guessed at least half of them were talking about Landon too. She leaned in closer to Brock.

"She said she slept with Frank Fisher."

"The director of *Starless Night?*"

"Yes. According to her, and to many a gossip column, Frank and Landon don't see eye to eye. Landon often caused trouble on set, and though Frank saw the talent in him, he wasn't happy with how difficult he made it to work. And, if Miranda's drunk ramblings are to be believed, Frank has also been lusting after her for quite some time. I think she saw it as an act of revenge, but maybe Frank sees the ball as being in his court now. If he cares for Miranda the way she implied he does, then I think it's entirely possible that he would do something drastic to the man that caused her such misery."

"And that could mean Franks's involved in Landon's disappearance…"

"He's got plenty of money in his pocket to pay someone to do his dirty work. Plus, he's got more than one reason to hate Landon: the man *ruined* his dream project. I think we need to dig deeper into this guy."

"I saw him earlier. There's a table of directors out back. He was being pretty loud, telling stories and making everyone hang off his every word," Brock said pointedly. "I think he's drunk enough now to broach the subject of Landon, don't you?"

"I think we should at least go and see," Olivia agreed. "He's one of the people we came here for. Have you seen Sebastian Morales tonight?"

"No. Yara said she hasn't spotted him either. She texted him, but he hasn't replied. She said that's not unusual for him though. I believe they had a fling a while ago. He's been giving her the cold shoulder ever since."

"It's like a spider's web," Olivia murmured, slipping her arm through Brock's and allowing him to lead the way. Her feet were aching, but adrenaline kept her going. "Everyone seems to be connected here."

"Let's just hope we don't get too tangled in all of this. We don't have the money to hire a hit man if things go south and we anger the wrong people."

Olivia chuckled despite herself. It all seemed so ludicrous to her. The pettiness of it all, the high school drama that seemed to exist among these high-ranking and wealthy people. Was Yara right? Did people simply get bored and find drama to keep their lives interesting? Is that why Landon was missing?

Olivia could hear Frank Fisher before she could see him. He was telling jokes that weren't funny enough for the laughter they earned him. Olivia eyed him carefully, taking him in. He wasn't as she expected. He was relatively handsome, if a little plain, with dark brown hair and mischievous blue eyes. He sat dead center at a round table, a curved booth surrounding it, and he had a woman on either side of him, giggling at his every word. His arms were slung over the back of the chair, and he was a little slumped, looking drunker than he probably was. The table was full, and there were others hanging around, wishing to be in his circle. It seemed that Frank Fisher was a popular man.

He didn't notice as Brock and Olivia joined the crowd of people hanging on to his every word. *At least we blend in with his flock,* Olivia thought to herself. She forced herself to stand through some of his boring stories, pretending to laugh as she shifted from foot to foot. She was waiting and hoping for the subject of Landon Brown to surface, curious to see how Frank might respond.

Brock went off to fetch them some more drinks, leaving Olivia to hold down the fort. It had been almost half an hour of standing around, waiting for something to happen, but she seemed to be the only one getting bored. Not one single person went off to mingle or enjoy the night elsewhere. It seemed that all these people were desperate for an audience with Frank. She supposed that was what status and money had earned him, considering that he was the most boring man she'd ever had to listen to.

It was just as Brock returned that the subject shifted. Olivia was taking a grateful gulp of champagne when someone mentioned Landon's name. Frank latched on to the topic like a hook catching a fish.

"Landon … oh, Landon," he said with a theatrical sigh. "What a divisive figure. And now that he's gone, disappeared for a time, it seems he's all we can talk about. You know, I was probably the last person to see him."

"You were?" the young woman next to him gasped. Olivia's eyebrows raised. If he was, this was the first she had heard of it.

"Yes, I saw him just before the ceremony was about to begin. We had just walked the red carpet. He didn't say hello, of course. Not like I'd expect that man to."

Olivia narrowed her eyes. Why was Frank talking as if Landon was a dead man? And was he really so willing to talk so bitterly about him in public?

"He and I had lunch earlier that day too," Frank added, doing a quick sweep of the table with his eyes to ensure everyone was listening to him. Of course, they were. "We didn't tell anyone we were going… we didn't want the press involved. It was meant to be an opportunity for us to hash out our differences. Quaint little place. A roadside diner, completely off the map when you're used to fine dining. Damn good burger though. Anyway, I'm sure you have all heard that he and I had our… differences on set. The truth is, I wanted to find some common ground. I wanted to *help* him through whatever he was going through. I thought it would be nice to iron things out, to sweep our issues under the rug. But he can be difficult to get along with. I used whatever I could to make him promise he'd get some help—real help—but, you know. Not for him. Shame."

Isn't it strange how he went missing the same day you were unable to end your feud? Olivia mused silently. She thought there was something off about the way Frank was talking. Why was he so readily admitting that he didn't have a good relationship with a missing person? Given everything she knew, she could see how that was a spectacularly bad idea for him. But then again, he had no idea he was in the presence of two FBI agents. He was surrounded by people he thought were his adoring fans. He felt untouchable. Of course, he was willing to speak so brazenly about what was on his mind.

"What do you think happened to him?" one of the women at the table asked him, leaning in as if his answer was going to be so revolutionary that she couldn't possibly miss it. He sighed, leaning back in his chair.

"Well, ladies, I think it's safe to say that someone wanted him gone. I'm sure plenty of people did. And now they've succeeded. I don't know if he's dead or alive. I don't know if he's coming back or not. But the world keeps on turning. And now that the top dog is gone… who knows who might step into the limelight next?"

CHAPTER SEVEN

Olivia and Brock slunk away from Frank Fisher's table at around half past two. Olivia had heard more than enough coming out of his pompous mouth, and she was no closer to guessing what his game was. He clearly didn't care that Landon was missing, but he was also using it like some sort of self-promotion tactic. Four separate times, Olivia had heard him mention that he was the last person to see Landon before he disappeared, though it soon became clear that he, like hundreds of other people, simply saw him on the red carpet. He was keen to mention his meeting with him earlier that day, too, and to point out that whatever olive branch he'd extended to Landon hadn't been taken. He stayed away from details, though, and Olivia couldn't understand what he was hoping to gain. Was he trying to create intrigue about himself? Was he trying to make sure that people knew he was the good guy, and thus imply that he didn't do anything to hurt Landon?

Or, like a true narcissist, was he just happy to find a way to talk about himself?

"That man has no shortage of ego," Brock murmured as they made their escape. "What are your thoughts?"

"I honestly have no idea what to think. What about you?"

"I don't know either. He was name-dropping Landon left, right, and center. But he never once said they were friends, or that they were on good terms. Usually when someone is trying to misdirect blame from themselves, they talk positively about the missing or dead person, right?"

"Right. But I guess all press is good press. He's got a movie to promote, and since Landon was the star of it, maybe this is his way of worming his way to front page news. Maybe he hopes that the more he talks, the more likely it is that he'll be talked *about*."

"Entirely possible. Especially because there are a bunch of reporters milling around."

"There are?" Olivia said, glancing around the room. There were so many people around that it was hard to pin any of them down or identify them.

"Oh, they're sneaking around somewhere. Some of the actors and actresses here even pay columnists to spin a story about them. Yara says that it's a good way of getting your name into gossip magazines, if that's what you're into."

"That sounds organic," Olivia said sarcastically. "It reeks of desperation."

"I don't disagree. But we both know what it takes to climb the ladder. Sometimes, you have to demean yourself a little to get what you want."

Olivia thought about that for a moment. Would talking to a columnist get them somewhere with their investigation? Reporters were known for their eagle eyes. If they'd seen anything of interest, maybe they could be persuaded to talk about it.

"Maybe we should pay one of the columnists for information," Olivia whispered to Brock as they exited the conservatory. His eyes widened in shock and amusement.

"That's new, coming from you."

"I just think we're running out of things to do here, and we haven't learned as much as I was hoping we would. There's no sign of Sebastian Morales anywhere. Miranda is probably home by now puking her guts out. I can't stand to listen to Frank for another minute, and I think we've exhausted his usefulness for now. And the thing is, we can't be everywhere at once. Someone else who is looking for gossip might be our best chance at getting some answers."

"Maybe. But we're supposed to be laying low. Do we really want to be paying off the press and drawing attention to ourselves? Nothing shouts cops louder than slipping cash on the sly."

"We'll make it a part of our alibi," Olivia offered. "If a lot of up-and-coming nobodies pay the press to spin stories, why can't they be paid to tell them before the world finds out? Is it so far-fetched?"

Brock considered her for a moment. "Maybe you're right. Okay then, let's do it. I think I know where to start. Yara was talking about a particular guy earlier, Grayson Worth. Apparently he had some sort of arrangement with Landon. He knows things about people before they know them themselves."

"Spooky. How will we find him?"

"Consider me found."

Olivia whirled around and saw a handsome young man looking back at her with a smug smile playing on his lips. He blended right into the crowd of the rich and famous, dressed well in an asymmetrical zig-zag suit that left parts of his skin exposed. He had tanned skin and a stylish amount of stubble across his strong jaw, and a pair of thick-framed glasses were propped on the end of his nose. Olivia suspected that the lenses were fake from the way he wore them slightly farther down his nose.

"How long have you been listening to us?" Brock asked warily. Grayson cocked his head to the side.

"Since you started talking about cops. Don't worry. Your secret is safe with me. But you already know the drill about... *slipping cash on the sly.*"

Brock sighed and took his wallet out of his jacket. Grayson batted his hand away.

"Not here," he said, frowning. "I know a place we can talk. Follow me."

Olivia glanced at Brock. She sensed danger here. But it was a little late to bail now that they'd been exposed to Grayson. They followed him through the long hallways. Famous faces scowled at Grayson as he passed through, which could only mean one thing: he was well-known in the worst possible way. He'd likely ruined lives and saved them with his articles. That amount of power put Olivia right on the edge. They couldn't afford to blow the case, and certainly not so soon.

The rooms got quieter as they moved through them, and they soon came to what looked like a broom closet. But when Grayson opened the door, they found a small spiral staircase leading upward. Grayson put a finger to his lips.

"Our little secret," he said with an amused smile. "We won't be disturbed up here."

"How the hell do you know about this?" Brock asked as they cautiously followed Grayson upward. He laughed, the sound echoing a little in the small entryway.

"I know everything. Close the door behind you, Olivia."

Olivia didn't even want to know how the man knew her name, and she certainly didn't want to give him the satisfaction of asking. She headed up after the other two and found herself met by the chill of the night air. They were standing on a private balcony, overlooking the house gardens. Grayson sighed, the wind rushing through his hair.

"A little colder than I'd like, but I understand the need for discretion here. I understand you're working Landon Brown's disappearance case?"

"Who told you?" Brock asked sharply. Grayson tsked.

"You think you're so smart, snooping around in our territory like you can just fit in. I know a narc when I see one, okay? And you two show up on the arm of Yara Montague several days after a major A-lister goes missing? Please. Could you be *any* more obvious?"

Olivia's heart seized in her chest. If Grayson told anyone, they wouldn't be able to continue with their method of investigation. But he just smiled at them knowingly.

"I'm sorry. But rest assured—I don't intend to out you. I just figured we can help one another out. You tell me what you know, and I'll tell you what I know in return."

That was a deal Olivia wasn't willing to make. She refused to air Miranda's problems to the world when she'd worked so hard to keep a lid on her domestic issues. It wasn't her story to tell to anyone who didn't need to hear it. She stayed quiet, trying to figure out what cheap information she could give Grayson to get him to talk. He raised an eyebrow at her.

"I can see you considering the ways in which you can lowball me. And that's fine. If you want to play that game, I'll play it back. You'll get what you give."

This man is impossibly good, Olivia thought to herself. Grayson smirked at her as if he'd read her mind.

"I know I'm good. I've been doing this a long time. Now, if you're done with the games, we can talk properly."

Olivia took a deep breath. "Fine. We don't know all that much... but we listened to Frank Fisher talking for a while. He seems like he might have something to hide. He kept talking about Landon, saying he was the last person to see him before he disappeared."

"That so? I've got half of Hollywood telling me the same thing," Grayson countered. "It's a little claim to fame, I suppose... to be the last person to see an A-lister alive."

"Nobody said he's dead," Brock said, his jaw tense. Grayson raised an eyebrow.

"Right you are. But what is it that you always say in your line of work? That if a person isn't found within the first forty-eight hours of going missing, they're usually dead?"

"That's a myth," Olivia said, "but irrelevant. Our job is to find out what happened to him and why, not to figure out if he's dead or not. Who else has said they saw him last?"

"Oh, anyone who is anyone. Including myself. I last glimpsed him as he was walking the red carpet, along with hundreds of others. Landon and I have crossed paths a number of times, so I was quite pleased to see him. But he wasn't himself that evening, as I'm sure many will tell you. He looked unwell. Sickly. Depressed, perhaps. I suppose going through a divorce is never easy on the heart."

"He met with Frank Fisher earlier that day," Olivia said. "Perhaps that might have something to do with it."

"Interesting. You've managed to tell me something I didn't know," Grayson chuckle. "Color me impressed. I guess I can give you something that I won't be publishing in my column… but might be of use to you. I trust this information won't go any further than you and your superiors?"

"Yes, of course," Olivia said urgently. Grayson nodded.

"You might be interested to know that Landon Brown and Miranda Morgan weren't simply going through a divorce because of his infidelity. She recently brought evidence of abuse to the table."

Olivia tried not to look disappointed. Perhaps that information would've been useful a few hours ago, but it was nothing that Miranda hadn't already told her. Grayson seemed to clock Olivia's expression.

"Ahh. You already knew. I suppose you must've had quite a cozy chat with Mrs. Morgan when you were helping her escape this God-awful party."

Brock threw up his hands in frustration. "It's like you're everywhere at once! How did you know about that?"

"Oh please, enough of the drama. I saw her escort Miranda to her car."

"Well, how on earth did you know about her abuse allegations?"

"I told you. Landon and I have crossed paths a number of times," Grayson said cagily. "I told you something. So now you return the favor."

"Hang on a second. You didn't tell us anything we didn't already know," Olivia pointed out. "This isn't a fair exchange."

"If you're not willing to tell me anything else, then I'm afraid our conversation is over."

"This is a missing persons investigation. Don't you care about that? I thought you and Landon were friends?"

"Friends is not the word I would use to describe our relationship. I'm a reporter, Miss Knight. I don't have many friends at all. And as much as I hope you find him, I'm a businessman. I deal in secrets or cash. If you don't have either to offer me, then I have nothing to offer you."

Olivia didn't often dislike a person so quickly after meeting them, but Grayson was a slippery man. Still, she could see how they might need him, and they might also need to keep him quiet. If money was the way they got answers, they might have to be willing to pay him off. Brock caught her eye and nodded, confirming her own thoughts. She turned back to Grayson.

"We don't have cash on us. But would you be willing to exchange numbers? We'll pay you for good information," Olivia offered. Grayson smirked.

"Ahh. A businesswoman too. I like that. And it's a proposition I'll definitely consider. How about you take my card, and I'll take your number? I am sure we can be of use to one another again soon."

Olivia reluctantly took the deal, inputting her number into Grayson's phone. He smiled as she handed it back to him.

"A pleasure doing business with you. And as a gesture of goodwill, I'll tell you something that I'm sure you're dying to know. Sebastian Morales isn't here tonight, and with good reason."

"And I suppose you're not going to tell us what that reason is?" Brock said bitterly.

"Of course not. I can't do *all* the legwork for you. You're the cops here, not me. Good luck with the investigation. I'm sure we will be in touch again."

Grayson descended the stairs, leaving them with a jaunty wave. As soon as he was gone, Brock let out a grunt.

"I hope I never have to see that man again."

Olivia sighed. "Something tells me we will."

CHAPTER EIGHT

I T WAS NEARLY FOUR IN THE MORNING WHEN BROCK AND Olivia arrived back at Yara's house. She had insisted that they go on without her, her grin splitting her face as she threw back yet another glass. Olivia let out a long, tired sigh, watching LA pass them by as Yara's driver took them back.

"I don't know how she does this all the time," Olivia said. "I'm exhausted."

"That does tend to happen when you're the only person not drinking in a crowded room of drunk people," Brock chuckled. He reached for her hand. "Still, it was an experience. I don't think we will go to many parties like that in our lifetime."

"I don't think I mind that too much. Once was enough. Especially given that the night was hardly a success."

"I don't see it that way. You got good information from Miranda. We know a little more about Frank. And now we know to watch out for Grayson Worth too. Not bad for the first night of an investigation."

"I guess that's true," Olivia said. She did have a tendency to be hard on herself. She thought of Miranda and hoped that she was alright. After the night she'd had, Olivia would be surprised if she remembered anything by morning, but Olivia would never forget crossing paths with Miranda Morgan. A memory like that was sure to stick in her mind. Was she one of the first people in the world to learn that a famous actress had been trapped in an abusive relationship for so long?

When Olivia and Brock arrived back at Yara's house, they thanked the driver and let themselves in. The grand building was quiet without Yara's presence, and Olivia felt like that made the place bigger. It was a little intimidating, standing in the kind of place she would never own herself. It felt like every step she took needed to be careful, like she was dirtying the place just by being there. She finally slipped off her heels, her feet aching as she placed them flat on solid ground. She groaned.

"I don't think I'm cut out for this life. I never want to wear heels again."

"But you look so good in them," Brock said, only half teasing. They headed upstairs and Olivia hitched her dress so that she wouldn't trip over it. Only now did she consider how expensive the gown was. Probably more than she made in a year. She was glad to only be having this revelation now, or she would've been an anxious mess all evening trying not to ruin it somehow.

The bedroom that Yara had directed them to was bigger than Brock's old apartment back home and housed little more than a king-sized bed and a dressing table. As Olivia got ready for bed, she took it all in, wondering what it must be like to own such a place, to know that they had riches beyond compare.

"Have you ever wanted a life like this?" Olivia asked Brock. "A life where you don't have to worry about money… where everything is easier and life always seems to be on your side?"

Brock slid into the bed, considering the question. "I don't think so."

"Really?"

"Well, yeah. I don't think that sounds very exciting. I know some people grow up dreaming of a career that will make them rich, or marrying into wealth, or inheriting a small fortune from a long-lost uncle... but I guess ever since everything went down with my grandfather, my dreams have always been more... domestic."

"In what sense?"

Brock smiled at Olivia. "Well, for starters, I've found a job I love. It might not make me millions, but I love what I do, and that's enough for me. I think I always prioritized the idea of an interesting job over a well-paying one. But the most important thing to me doesn't involve work. For me... I've been waiting to find my person... to fall in love and build a life with her." His eyes softened as he gazed at Olivia. "And now that's falling into place too."

Olivia blushed at the implication. She knew deep down that that's what they were doing—building a life together. And she wanted that too. It was just a little scary to know that was the path they were on. It was so much more serious than casually dating. And ever since Jean had mentioned marriage, it had been on her mind even more. How long would it be before she reached that stage in her life? And when it arrived, would she be ready this time?

"The thing is though... I recognize when the person I'm with isn't ready for the next step yet," Brock said, entwining his fingers with Olivia's. "I know how to pace a relationship. And no part of me is in a rush to do everything at once. You don't need to worry, Olivia. I'm not diving in headfirst. I know where I'm at, and I know where you're at. And I know we'll get to the same point someday. I know we have a future together. I'm sorry if that scares you."

"It doesn't," Olivia said quickly. "But I'm scared of messing that up. I've already had one failed engagement."

"Did you love him the way you love me?"

Olivia paused before shaking her head. "No. I've never loved anyone the way I love you."

Brock's soft smile turned into a grin. Olivia clicked her tongue. "Don't be smug, now."

"I can't help it. You're just so good at feeding my ego."

Olivia chuckled. "I guess I am. But it's true. And I don't want to screw that up. I… I'm sorry if my mom freaked you out with what she said. She certainly freaked me out a bit."

"That's alright. Parents tend to be good at that."

"Yeah, you're not wrong." Olivia sighed. "And I guess coming here has been challenging for me in a way. I know I shouldn't compare our pasts, but with my previous engagement, and your relationship with a movie star… I just question the paths our lives could have taken. You could be a millionaire now with a fancy house and a fancy girlfriend."

"And you could be married to some boring dud who doesn't have a sense of humor."

Olivia swatted Brock playfully, and he laughed before pulling her in closer to him, kissing the top of her head. Olivia shook her head.

"You know what I'm saying. It's impossible not to think about when we're staying in your ex-girlfriend's house. I know it's ancient history, and I know you don't care about her the way you care about me. It's just on my mind."

"I know. You overthink everything, and it's not your fault. You have every reason to when things haven't worked out in the past. But everything happens for a reason. You and me, right here right now… this was meant to happen. Everything leading up to this was to give us a chance at our moment together. You don't need to worry anymore. There's nothing standing in our way."

Olivia felt her heart warm in her chest. She leaned in and kissed Brock, feeling finally content with their position. Nothing was rushing them. Nothing was blocking their path. What would be would be.

"I love you," she murmured.

"I love you too. But if I don't get to sleep soon, I'm going to be so damn cranky in the morning."

Olivia groaned. "Even I'm not relishing the idea of getting up for this case. That party has worn me out."

"Not to worry. I hear that LA doesn't come alive until lunch time. Let's sleep in a little before we get to work. And then I think we need to hunt down our first interviewee."

"Who?"

"Sebastian Morales."

CHAPTER NINE

O LIVIA WOKE UP AT 10:30 A.M. WITH A HEADACHE AND A dry mouth. She groaned. It was typical that she had barely drank anything and she still ended up with the effects of a hangover. Brock was still fast asleep next to her, so she got up and headed to the bathroom to take a shower. The house was quiet as she enjoyed the hot water, and Olivia suspected that every person who had attended the party the night before was either fast asleep or straight-up passed out. But fortunately for them, the person they wanted to speak with hadn't been in attendance.

Olivia wondered what reason Sebastian Morales would have to skip the party. He was a big shot in Hollywood, and he was no stranger to the party scene, just like all the other celebrities in the city. So, what would make him skip this party in particular? She was almost certain it had something to do with Landon's disappearance. Did he want to avoid looking guilty when everyone knew there was tension between the two of them?

Olivia thought about what Grayson had said last night: *Sebastian Morales isn't here tonight… and with good reason.* That had to mean something; Grayson certainly thought it was useful information. What piece of the puzzle were they missing? Was there more to the tension between the two rival actors than met the eye?

As Olivia was getting out of the shower, Brock was just waking up. He stretched and groaned, shaking his head.

"I'm getting too old for these late nights," he muttered. "Why do I feel like someone hit me in the head with a brick? I didn't even drink that much…"

"That's sleep deprivation," Olivia said, pulling on some clothes from her suitcase. "Come on, let's start making moves. Hopefully Yara will be awake soon. She said she'd be able to get us access to all areas, right? Do you think she will be able to get us a visit with Sebastian?"

"I think Yara can do anything she wants. She certainly acts like she can," Brock said with an affectionate roll of his eyes. "But I'll bet she's only just gone to bed. We might have trouble getting ahold of her."

But when they headed downstairs twenty minutes later, both of them ready for the day, they were shocked to find Yara lounging on the sofa, her face covered in a slimy green face mask and her hair wrapped in a towel. She was sipping what looked like a mimosa, and there was a platter of pastries on the table in front of her. She grinned when she saw Olivia and Brock approaching and raised her glass to them.

"Good morning! Did you sleep well?"

"Did *you*?!" Brock exclaimed. "What time did you get home?"

"Oh, like seven. Enough time for a power nap. And now it's time to seize the day!"

"How are you not horribly hungover? Olivia and I are suffering, and we didn't even drink…"

"It's called hair of the dog," Yara said with a mischievous smile. She sipped her mimosa. "More alcohol and a little Vitamin C. I'll be all good by noon."

"I don't know how you do it."

Yara shrugged. "I'm well trained. Both of you sit. Have a croissant. Would you like a mimosa too?"

"Better not," Olivia said warily, sitting down and picking a pastry from the platter along with a side plate. "We're hoping to speak to Sebastian Morales today."

"I think he might be out of town. I didn't see him last night," Yara said.

"We think he might have been avoiding the party," Brock said. "We spoke to Grayson Worth. He said—"

Yara scoffed. "You don't want to trust a man like Grayson Worth. He loves selling people out left, right, and center."

"That's sort of useful to us," Olivia said carefully. "No one likes a snitch, but his information was good, from what he told us. He said that Sebastian had good reasons to not be at the party last night. That means we need to talk to him."

"Hmm," Yara mused as she bit into a pastry, spilling crumbs onto her lap. She didn't seem to care much that she was making a mess. "There's no denying that his absence was noticeable. I would've thought he'd be celebrating being rid of Landon for at least a bit. They weren't exactly best buddies. But maybe that's not a good look and he thought better of it. With Landon out of the picture, the world would be in the palm of Sebastian's hand."

"So, you think he could've done something to hurt Landon?"

Yara considered the question for a moment before shaking her head. "No. Sebastian's a good guy. I went on a date with him once. We weren't a good match. He was kind of boring."

Brock raised an eyebrow. "Kind of boring? Or *you* were too much?"

Yara smiled but didn't clarify. "He was so calm and patient with me... I can't see him doing anything to hurt anyone. He might be fighting for his own career, but I don't think he'd make a man disappear to make it to the top. He's still doing pretty well for himself."

"Hmm. I think we should still talk to him," Brock said. "I would like to at least hear his thoughts on Landon. They worked closely together on their latest movie. He's got to have some thoughts on the man and his life. Maybe he would have some insight into a catalyst that might have caused this mess."

Yara shrugged. "Suit yourself. Want me to call him? I can tell him that you're private investigators looking into the disappearance of Landon."

"Maybe don't mention us. Just ask if you can come over. I doubt he'll agree to let two private investigators into his house. Or FBI agents, for that matter," Olivia said.

Yara nodded. "Alright. Give me an hour or two."

"Thank you, Yara. We really appreciate this," Brock said.

Yara smiled. "Should be fun."

Yara swanned off with her mimosa, and Olivia watched her go with a stab of sadness in her heart. All that money and time on her hands, and Yara still had nothing better to do than to help them out. It seemed a lonely existence to her, waking up alone after a raging party and drinking more to get through the day. Olivia caught Brock's eye, and she could see concern in his eyes too. Yara might be bubbly and excitable on the outside, but something told Olivia that the perfect life she pretended to have might not be so perfect after all.

But it wasn't her place to judge. She barely knew Yara, and she'd been a very sweet and welcoming host. She couldn't make assumptions about her after only twenty-four hours in her presence. It was the weekend, after all, and Yara had every right to party every week. It didn't mean that her life was falling apart.

But when they finally got into the car to head to Sebastian's home, Olivia could smell the liquor on Yara, who crowded into the backseat with them. She linked her arm through Olivia's like they were old girlfriends, and her head lolled ever so slightly to the side.

"It's so nice to have you guys around," she remarked with a smile. "I don't get many visitors these days. Life gets busy, doesn't it?"

Olivia felt her stomach twist. Was she imagining the loneliness she was sure she detected in Yara? Was she making up a story about her, or was there some truth to it?

Yara chuckled to herself at absolutely nothing, making Olivia exchange a glance with Brock. She was clearly still drunk.

"Hey, Yara … why don't we all have dinner together tonight? Just the three of us?" Olivia offered with a warm smile. "You can sleep off your hangover this afternoon and then we can grab some food … or I could cook!"

Yara laughed. "I wouldn't even know how to use most of the things in my kitchen, but if you'd like to tackle using them, go ahead! Dinner sounds lovely, but don't you worry about little old me. I know you two are here for work. I'm sure you'll be very busy."

"Not too busy for dinner," Brock said with a smile. "You know I don't miss meals."

Yara smiled. "Well, then … I guess we're on. But as for sleeping off the hangover, I'm fine. Really, I am."

Olivia wasn't convinced, but she didn't want to say anything further. She just hoped that Yara was capable of taking care of herself. She also hoped she would be able to hold up while they were visiting Sebastian. They needed her to convince Sebastian that they could be trusted, that he could speak to them openly. It was a risky move, interviewing him when they still hoped to lay low, but Olivia knew it was unlikely that Sebastian would tell anyone about their visit. Being visited by two FBI agents was never a good look. If Sebastian was also trying to lay low, then he would definitely keep quiet about their meeting.

Sebastian's house was just as grand as Yara's, if not more so, but it had a more unkempt feel to it. Yara confirmed her identity at the gates, and they were let through. The property was surrounded by beautiful foliage and wildflowers, like the place was just left to its own devices. Olivia liked seeing so much greenery in a city of concrete and neon lights. She could see why Sebastian might like it too. It kept anyone who might be passing by from seeing in. It protected his privacy, even if only a little bit.

Sebastian was waiting on the doorstep in a robe, looking a little worse for wear. His handsome face was marred by tiredness, dark circles under his eyes, and a few days' worth of stubble on his jaw. He didn't look shocked when Olivia and Brock followed Yara out of the car, as if he'd been expecting some kind of setup. Yara threw her arms around Sebastian for a hug, which he received stiffly, not taking his eyes off the two strangers before him.

"I should've guessed you'd pull something, Yara," Sebastian muttered, looking Olivia up and down like she was a dirty dishrag.

"You're so paranoid, Sebastian," Yara drawled, clearly not taking the moment very seriously at all. "This is my childhood boyfriend, Brock, and his beautiful girlfriend. They're simply lovely, and I just had to introduce them to you."

"How thoughtful," Sebastian said, finally pushing Yara off him. "But I know why you're here. I don't hear from you in months, Yara, and then all of a sudden you turn up with a couple of strangers? *FBI agents*, you said? Right in the middle of Landon Brown disappearing?"

"It's true. We're agents from the FBI," Brock said, supplying his badge. "But Yara didn't lie. I am her ex. And my girlfriend truly is beautiful."

Sebastian rolled his eyes. "How touching. But I still don't understand the need for you to be on my property."

"We just want to talk a little," Olivia attempted. "A man has disappeared. You worked closely with him recently. We're just hoping for a little insight into the man he is, who might want him gone, that kind of thing. If you can spare an hour of your time…"

"Well, it doesn't feel like I have much of a choice in the matter, so I suppose you'd better come inside," Sebastian said stiffly, stepping aside to allow them in.

"Thank you," Olivia said, trying to remain polite. There was no sense in angering him further. He had every right to be irritated by the entrance they'd made, but they also had every right to be questioning him. The better he cooperated, the better it would be for everyone.

Sebastian led them through his home, and Olivia inhaled the smell of flowers in the air. There were vases of gorgeous arrangements on almost every surface, and there were paintings of flowers all over the walls. It was beautiful and elegant, a home that

Olivia thought anyone would be lucky to live in. As they entered the living room, Sebastian caught her looking at the paintings. He sat down, fiddling with an arrangement on his coffee table.

"My parents were florists before they retired," he said. "And they passed their love on to me. I would have been one too if I hadn't gone into acting."

"The flowers are beautiful," Brock said, taking a seat opposite Sebastian. "Thank you for allowing us into your home. We understand this must make you uncomfortable."

Sebastian shook his head. "I'm used to being uncomfortable. This life in Hollywood ... it was never for me. I don't belong here. I try to hide from it all."

"The lights and glamour too much?" Brock asked.

Sebastian chuckled softly. "I love my job, but the price that comes with it ... I'll never know true peace. There's always some scandal going on. And now with Landon gone ... I knew someone would come talk to me eventually. You all read the tabloids. You assume we're the worst enemies from the articles you read."

Yara laughed at the notion, slumping down on the sofa beside him. "Oh, Sebastian. Worst enemies? Really? You make it sound like a movie ..."

"And so does the media. You think they don't overexaggerate everything for the public's entertainment? Yes, Landon and I struggled to see eye to eye ... we are very different characters. But I am not his enemy, and he is not mine. We're simply not ... friends."

Olivia nodded to let him know she was hearing his thoughts. She could understand how things could get blown out of proportion. And for a man like Sebastian, who clearly liked his own space, what was the sense in fighting against every rumor he heard? He would only add fuel to the fire. Still, he was connected to Landon whether he liked it or not. The world would speculate no matter what he said or did.

So, if he had nothing to hide, he could be truly honest with them.

"When did you last see Landon?" Olivia asked. "I presume you saw him at the show?"

"Everyone saw him at the show," Sebastian said, a tinge of bitterness in his voice. "And everyone chose to overlook his awful state that evening. He was drunk, but no one seems to be mentioning that. It would ruin his big comeback story if his fans knew he'd been getting wasted the whole time. I saw enough of that on the set of *Starless Night*. But before that night, I hadn't seen him in some time. It was probably some press event for the movie, but I don't fully recall. I stayed out of his way mostly, and he stayed out of mine. It was for the best."

Olivia nodded. "I understand. And what can you tell us about his behavior on set with Miranda? And Frank Fisher?"

Sebastian sniffed. "Well, he and Miranda weren't on good terms on set. Obviously. But Miranda handled it with grace. She didn't have to, after the way she was treated, but she is a good woman. I admired her for that. As for Frank... I don't know what you know about that man, but he doesn't truly have any friends."

"Is that so?" Olivia asked. He seemed to have plenty of friends at the party the night before.

"Yes. He's always surrounded by people, but I wouldn't describe them as his friends. I'd call them his followers. People always swarm around him because he has power, and everyone seems to want a piece of it. If you follow movies at all, you'll know he dominates the silver screen with his work. Everyone wants to be in his films, even if he's dishing out more flops these days than successes. That's just how it is. It's the reason I chose to work on *Starless Night*. Landon and Miranda, too, despite everything going on between them. But the biggest issue on set was always the feud between Frank and Landon."

"Can you tell us more about that?"

"Look... I'm not the biggest fan of either of them, but Frank was very difficult to work for. He wanted everything to be *exact*. This was his big masterpiece, the thing he'd been wanting to make for years. Landon, on the other hand... well, you know his reputation. He got back on the wagon pretty much immediately. Said he was 'method acting.' It made him a nightmare to work with because he wouldn't conform to how Frank wanted things to be. And if you've seen the movie, it shows. The whole thing was a mess. Landon acted well… except it wasn't really acting. He was just lost in the role. And it made a lot of people angry because he's not a good drunk. He kept saying he was in character… but how do you separate his character from the man he really is when he's wasted on set?"

"It sounds complicated."

"It sounds like showbiz to me," Yara snickered. "Landon's always been this way. Frank should've known better than to hire him if he couldn't handle the heat."

"It's not my place to comment," Sebastian said blandly. "What you're really asking me is if I think either of them would have done something to him. Miranda? No. Absolutely not. Frank? I wouldn't put it past him. Especially since things clearly didn't go well between him and Landon when they met up before the show."

Olivia paused on that note. Sebastian was still talking, but what he said had caught her attention. Frank had implied that the meeting was kept low-key, which is why they'd gone to a tiny diner off the beaten track. He'd implied that no one knew about that meeting until Frank gossiped about it following Landon's disappearance.

So how did Sebastian know about it?

Olivia's heart was beating hard in her chest. Something was amiss. Sebastian hadn't even been at the party to hear Frank going on about it. He claimed that Frank had no friends, so it was unlikely they kept in touch. So, in that case, how had Sebastian come to know about a secret meeting he wasn't a part of?

Olivia had to pose the question.

"How did you know?" she asked, cutting Sebastian off in his tracks. He paused, blinking several times.

"How did I know what?"

"About Frank and Landon's meeting. Frank said that it was kept private, until he talked about it at the party. You claim not to be friends with him or Landon. So how did you know about it?"

A look of pure horror crossed Sebastian's face. He clearly wasn't a good enough actor to hide his true feelings. He could see he'd slipped up. Yara was staring in shock at Sebastian, clearly trying to figure out what was going on. Sebastian stood abruptly, averting his gaze.

"I'd like you all to leave now."

"Mr. Morales…"

"I'm *telling* you to leave. I didn't invite you here. You're on my property without permission. I won't say anything further until I've spoken to my lawyer."

Olivia's face hardened. "Would you like us to return with a warrant, Sebastian? Because we can do that and make a scene, if you'd like."

"Or you can tell us right now what's going on," Brock finished. Sebastian wavered. He was like a wild animal caught in a trap.

"Out. Now."

"Seb…" Yara began, but he turned his back on her.

"Yara, I don't want to hear from you again. You've brought trouble to my doorstep, which I really don't appreciate. Get out, all of you."

Olivia wasn't going to fight it further. She knew what she needed to know: Sebastian Morales had something to hide, and he wasn't willing to tell them what it was. As they were herded from his home, Olivia knew one thing for certain.

She would get to the bottom of what Sebastian was hiding from them.

CHAPTER TEN

"**H**E'S GUILTY OF SOMETHING. THAT MUCH IS CLEAR," Olivia said.

They were back in Yara's private car, and she had agreed to drop them off at the venue of the show so they could interview some of the staff on duty that evening. Olivia was still reeling from their encounter with Sebastian, and it was making her shift uncomfortably in her seat. He was hiding something from them, and she needed to know what before it drove her crazy.

"It was weird," Yara whispered. "I've never seen him so... cagey. The Sebastian I know is a very open man. Are you sure he's involved with Landon's disappearance?"

"We don't know that," Brock said pointedly with a look in Olivia's direction. "But I can say one thing for sure: there's something he doesn't want us to know. I can tell from meeting him that he's a private man, but there's clearly something going on. I'd like to find out what."

"It might not be what you think," Yara said, worry seeping into her voice. "I just can't picture him doing anything cruel. So what if he knew that Landon and Frank were meeting?"

"I'm sorry, Yara, but we can't dismiss it. It's too important. You saw the way he responded. He knew we'd caught him in a lie. And now, we're going to have to dig deeper and figure out what he won't tell us."

"But he's not going to get into trouble, is he?"

Olivia turned away from Yara. She didn't want to have to explain to her that knowing someone and loving someone didn't make them a good person. She wasn't sure what Sebastian Morales was hiding, but it couldn't be anything good. The sooner they could go off on their own to investigate, the better. The last thing a woman as seemingly fragile as Yara needed was to get sucked into a missing person's case.

"Let's hope not," Brock said gently, clearly thinking the same thing. Olivia understood the need to appease at this point. They needed Yara to stay calm, or she might run her mouth and say something she shouldn't. That would complicate things even more.

Yara dropped them off at the venue and waved to them from the window, but her mood had clearly dampened since their visit to Sebastian. Brock let out a long sigh, seemingly glad to be away from Yara. He and Olivia walked toward the venue together.

"She doesn't seem like she's doing well," Brock murmured. "Do you think I should be worried?"

"I don't know. I don't know her well enough to judge," Olivia replied. "But the fact that you're worried tells me she's not right at the moment."

Brock shook his head. "The last time I saw her, she was nothing like this. Still a little extravagant, sure, but she wasn't drunk all the time. She had friends around her all the time, and she seemed … happy. Really happy. What do you think has changed?"

"I don't know. But it could easily be a product of her environment. We've only been here a day, and I'm already feeling suffocated by it all. I don't like the way things run here, Brock. It doesn't feel right."

"I know, I feel the same. Let's hope we get some answers soon. I don't want to stay here any longer than we have to. But before we leave, I need to talk to Yara properly. Make sure she's doing okay."

Olivia reached out to squeeze his hand. "You're a good friend."

"No, I'm not. If I was a good friend, I would've noticed this sooner. She's been perfectly curating her life for years, never letting anyone see the real her. I thought maybe it was just because she was having so much fun out here … but now I wonder if she's isolating herself. Her behavior doesn't seem normal to me. Happy people don't drink alone in the morning."

"You couldn't have known. But you're here now. I know you'll do everything to make sure she's okay. And I will too."

"Thanks, Olivia," Brock whispered. There was a small crack in his voice, and Olivia knew how much he cared for Yara. It was good to see this side of him—the side that gave up his emotions so easily. But she worried for him too. She didn't like to see him hurting. Still, they had work to do. She told herself that later that day, she would check in on him and see how he was coping with it all.

Inside the building felt oddly eerie. It was still set up for the awards night, with mess still scattered across the floor and the tables. The police had come and closed the scene, but not soon enough to prevent the show from going on, apparently. The cleaning staff were milling around, but they didn't seem in much of a hurry to get things done. They were all chatting among themselves in low voices, no doubt gossiping about what had happened under that very roof to Landon Brown.

But speaking to them wasn't the priority. They were looking for the stage manager on duty the night of Landon's disappearance. From their brief with Jonathan, they knew the stage manager was probably the last person to see Landon before he disappeared. Olivia approached one of the cleaners.

"Hi. We're looking for Megan Dean? We'd like to talk to her about a few things."

The cleaner, a stern looking woman in her late fifties, shrugged. "I don't know her personally. But there's a team briefing in the staff room for the stage crew. She's probably there."

"That's very helpful. Thank you. Can you point us in the right direction?"

They made their way through the building just in time to see a group of people filing out of the staff room. Olivia caught the eye of an official-looking woman who seemed to be the one in charge and looked more than a little rattled.

"Hi. We're looking for Megan Dean. Can you tell us where we can find her?"

The woman's already anxious expression turned to complete terror. "Am I in trouble?"

"No, not at all," Olivia said gently. "You're Megan?"

"Yes, that's me. Is this about … about …"

"Landon Brown. Yes."

Megan let out a long breath. "I don't know what happened. I really don't. Please don't arrest me."

"It's alright—no one is here to arrest you," Brock said firmly. "We just want to ask you a few questions about that night. We're trying to paint a picture of what went down."

Megan calmed herself with a deep breath, nodding slowly. "Okay. Yeah, I can do that."

"Wonderful. Is there somewhere we can go to speak in private?"

Megan swallowed. "Yes, of course … follow me."

Megan led them through the crowd of people exiting the staff room and then ducked inside the room, directing them to follow. She practically collapsed onto a sofa, like her legs simply wouldn't hold her up any longer. Olivia sat down, too, offering her a kind smile.

"Take a breath, Megan. This won't take long," she said gently. "We just want to hear your version of events."

"I've already spoken to the police about this …"

"We're not with the police. We're from the FBI," Brock said. "We've been assigned Landon Brown's case."

Megan's eyes widened. "The FBI? Oh man, I'm in way too deep…"

"Megan, that's not the case. This is just a casual conversation to help us learn more about the night he disappeared," Olivia said. "So, can you start by telling us what your role was on the night and how it related to Landon?"

Megan swallowed again before nodding anxiously. "Okay. I'll try."

"Good. In your own time."

"I… I was very busy. The role of a stage manager is very demanding for big events such as awards shows. So many moving parts—so many things going on at once. I had to make sure that everyone was in the right place at the right time. It's usually not an issue. I'm very organized. But I found Landon hard to keep track of. He was supposed to be presenting the show but he was… distracted."

"He was drunk," Olivia supplied.

Megan nodded. "I thought he'd gone clean. But… yeah, he must have been drunk. He wasn't particularly professional. I knew he didn't really want to be there. But I was determined to keep him on track. I kept giving him warnings every five minutes about when he would be going on stage. Everything else was ready to go; everyone was where they were supposed to be. And with the final five-minute warning, Landon was ready to go too."

"You saw him backstage?"

"Yes. I remember distinctly. I walked past his dressing room and told him his cue time, and he seemed ready for it. And then he never made it to his spot backstage with one minute to go. I was called on my walkie talkie to investigate… but he was gone. At the time, I thought maybe he just got bored and wandered off. I don't think anyone would've put it past him. I was busy trying to find someone else to take his place. I managed to grab Sammy Rosehurst to do it, and he was given the envelopes to take on stage. At that point, I was just catching my breath, relieved that the show hadn't completely fallen apart."

"Were you angry with Landon for screwing it up?" Olivia asked.

"Of course. But I don't know the man. I was irritated from a professional standpoint, not a personal one…"

Megan paused, taking a shaky breath. "And then… Sammy read out the message on the card. And everything changed. I knew something had gone horribly wrong, and it happened on my watch."

Brock shook his head. "Whatever happened… it happened within the space of five minutes. That's a tiny time frame for someone to pull something like this off. Was anyone else present in that area of the stage?"

"No. Most of the stage management was occupied in lighting or sound. *I* had the responsibility of keeping the actors on track. But like I said, I was juggling a lot of balls. I trusted that Landon would be able to handle the five-minute warning. He knew he just had to go on stage when the music started."

"So, no one else was likely to have seen him?" Olivia asked. Megan shook her head, her face creased with worry.

"No. And as I said, we've all spoken to the police already… not one person saw him. And we have security cameras, of course, but they didn't pick anything up. Wherever he went… we'll never have footage of it."

"What happened when people realized he was missing?"

"Things moved slowly at first. The show went on while we were trying to look for him. It was hard to know how seriously to take the message. It seemed like a prank. But when it became clear he was gone… that was when there was talk of calling the police. And eventually, hours later, the police showed up. That's all I know."

Olivia nodded solemnly. They hadn't learned much that they didn't already know, but Olivia was sure that they could rule out the stage manager's involvement. She would have been far too visible, far too busy, and likely had dozens of witnesses to back her up. Besides, what need would she have to make a man disappear?

"Thank you for your time, Megan."

"I can go? I'm really not in trouble?"

"Of course, you can go. Thank you for talking with us."

Megan clearly couldn't get away fast enough. She stood and scampered away, back to work. Olivia turned to Brock.

"Well, that didn't open much up. What next?"

"While we're here, I think we should poke around a little," Brock said. "I'd like to see his dressing room. I assume it's been left untouched."

"Then let's start there."

CHAPTER ELEVEN

THE DRESSING ROOM WAS A MESS. OLIVIA SHOULD HAVE expected nothing less—she had heard horror stories of famous celebrities leaving behind a trail of destruction in their wake, content to allow cleaners to mop up after them. Still, the room was clearly untouched. Landon's suit jacket and tie were strewn over a chair, and there was a bottle of his cologne on the vanity.

There was a whole bunch of stage makeup scattered around, too, ready for his big performance of the night. He had a suitcase in the room which had been opened and items from inside were thrown around carelessly. It was almost a deliberate act of disrespect. Olivia was sure that he'd had no intention of cleaning up after himself.

Brock approached the chair, examining the suit jacket and tie. "It's cold outside," he said. "It has been for weeks. If he left of his own accord, would he have gone without a jacket to keep warm?"

Olivia processed that for a moment. He was right. If Landon had plans to make a dramatic exit, he still would likely have had things with him. Why leave his jacket behind?

"Maybe he took something warm from the suitcase. Seems strange that he wouldn't just take it with him if he were going somewhere…"

"I suppose it's harder to make a quick getaway with a suitcase slowing you down. If he left deliberately, he'd have traveled light. But it definitely seems like that's not what happened," Brock said.

Olivia felt a chill run down her spine.

Olivia donned a pair of gloves from her pocket, glancing around the room. "We know the police already took a few things into evidence… but I'd like to take a deeper look. You never know what they might have missed."

"Agreed. Let's make sure they haven't been sloppy."

They got to work searching the room, careful not to disturb things too much. Olivia wasn't leaving until she had examined every nook and cranny of the room. She checked under every piece of strewn clothing, in every drawer inside the vanity, and inside the wardrobe. She spent ten minutes feeling around blindly in the dark cupboard, searching for anything that might be out of place. A weapon, perhaps, or a hidden personal item.

But it seemed there was nothing to find. Most of the items in the room clearly belonged to Landon, and there didn't seem to be anything of importance missing. Olivia tossed around the idea in her head of someone stealing from him and getting caught, so perhaps they had to take drastic measures and get rid of Landon. But she was sure a stunt like this had to be much more calculated than that. Five minutes was a tiny window for someone to get him out of there.

Whatever had gone down that night was no accident. Olivia was certain it had been planned long ahead of time, whether by

Landon or by some faceless kidnapper they hadn't unveiled yet. Only time would tell.

But Olivia was beginning to think that the dressing room was a dead end. She had searched almost everywhere. She sighed as she checked behind the vanity. Her fingers brushed against layers of dust, making her cringe. But then her fingers came across something solid. Something hard. She closed her hand around it and pulled it out, holding it in the palm of her hand. Her jaw dropped when she saw what it was.

It was a ring. A very *expensive* ring. It had a huge diamond embedded on it, and it sparkled in the light. Olivia thought it was quite ugly, actually, but there was no denying its value. So, what was it doing behind a vanity table in Landon Brown's dressing room?

"Brock… you need to see this."

Brock bent down to see what Olivia had in her hand. He let out a long whistle.

"Wow. Now that's a diamond. Where did you find it?"

"It was literally thrown behind the vanity. Who would do something like that? You could probably buy a whole country for the price of this thing."

"It looks familiar… I'm sure I've seen it somewhere before," Brock mused. "Hang on a second…"

Brock took out his phone and began typing something. By the sharp intake of his breath, Olivia could tell he'd found something interesting. He showed her what was on his screen.

Right before her eyes was a picture of the ring. It was decorating a delicate hand in the photograph, and Olivia was almost sure she knew whose hand it was.

"Miranda?"

"Yes. It was her engagement ring. I knew I'd seen it before. There was quite a stir in the news about it when they got engaged. I can remember Yara texting me about it. It's worth several million."

"Then what is it doing *here?*"

"Well… Miranda and Landon aren't married anymore, are they? So, I'd guess Miranda doesn't want the ring anymore. Maybe she was trying to give it back to him."

"On the night of the awards show?" Olivia asked. "They've been broken up for some time… why that night? And if she gave it back to him… does that mean she was here? In his dressing room? Because it sounds to me like that puts her somewhere she really shouldn't have been…"

"You think it's suspicious?"

"I can't say that it's not. Imagine how that conversation might've gone… she came in here and threw the ring back in his face. A gift he gave her long ago. You can see how that might start a fight, especially if he was intoxicated. Maybe Miranda snapped. Maybe she'd been snapping for quite some time, but this was the last straw. She throws the ring. It means nothing to either of them anymore, the money isn't important to either of them… and then she does something to him. And no one was around to hear because it was in that five-minute window…"

"I don't know. It seems like a big stretch. All that in five minutes? And then she left evidence on the scene? It seems… rash."

"I would be rash, too, in her shoes, after everything he's put her through," Olivia countered. "But you're right. That five-minute window simply doesn't hold enough seconds for that scenario to pan out. But whatever happened… she was here. There's no other reason for her ring to be here. I don't imagine that Landon would carry it around with him. So that begs the question… why was she in her ex's dressing room on the night he disappeared?"

CHAPTER TWELVE

O LIVIA AND BROCK LEFT THE DRESSING ROOM AT exactly the wrong time. Coming down the hallway was a team of four security guards, each of them hulking and looking furious. Olivia wondered if they were there to kick them out, even though they had every right to be there. The one at the head of the pack pointed at them accusingly.

"You! What were you doing in there? No one is supposed to be in there."

Olivia reached into her pocket for her badge. "We're with the FBI. We're here investigating the case of Landon Brown."

"And who allowed you into the building?"

"We walked straight in," Brock said coolly. "Shouldn't the security team be on the doors if they don't want strangers to just wander in?"

The man huffed. "We've been very busy."

"I can imagine so. When a star goes missing under your watch, it's probably not a good look. You must be working overtime to fix this mess," Brock said, keeping his voice level. Olivia wasn't sure why he was goading them, but she decided to trust him and let him carry on. She was sure he had his reasons.

"Watch your mouth," the man snapped as he came to a halt in front of them. "You have no idea the kind of pressure we're under."

"FBI agents don't know pressure? Sounds about right," Brock said, stepping toward the man. "Now listen up. We have a job to do, same as you. So long as you cooperate, it looks like we're on the same side. You're not in trouble with us. We're just trying to map out the night and get an idea of what might have happened. The sooner you help us, the sooner we'll leave."

The man scowled at Brock. "What do you need from us?"

"Anything that might be useful. We'd like to hear your experiences of the night and see all your security footage."

The man wavered. "And then you'll leave?"

"As soon as we're done with our work here, yes."

The beefy man crossed his arms across his chest. "Alright. You have a deal. I'm Kurt. I'll speak for my team. The others have work to do, or we're going to be in even more trouble than we already are."

He nodded for the rest to continue their duties, and the other three men skirted past and went on their way. Olivia could see the lines of worry on Kurt's face, and now Olivia understood Brock's method of dealing with him. He was trying to intimidate him to get him to be more talkative. And clearly, Kurt already felt he was in trouble by the way he was acting. Was his job on the line for what had happened to Landon under his protective watch? Was he worried about losing his job?

"You can follow me to the security office," Kurt said, walking off and leaving the two of them to follow him. "Not sure how much help I can be. Police didn't find anything."

"We appreciate it anyway," Olivia said.

Kurt nodded. "Whole thing's just a damned mess. Not sure I can dig myself out of this one."

"Your boss isn't happy with you?" Brock asked.

"No one is. Yes, we worked security that night, but our job was to oversee from the *outside*, not the inside. My team was responsible for keeping the crowds outside in check, manning the doors, making sure only the right people got inside. And when I tell you we did that job perfectly, that's not an exaggeration. No one got inside this building without our say-so. We screened everybody who arrived earlier in the day too… the catering staff, the ushers, the permanent staff here like the cleaners and the stage crew. If there was anyone inside the building who had something planned for Landon Brown, they didn't sneak in. I'd stake my reputation on it."

"You said you were manning the front of the building. What about the back of it?"

"There's only one exit out the back of the building: a fire escape. There are two side entrances, too, but one goes through the kitchens and the other the janitor's office. No one could've left that way without someone seeing them. The fire exit is in the main hall, in case of an emergency. A few of the seat fillers were on the security team, but they were situated in the main hall too. So, whatever happened to Landon, it happened backstage. There were people milling around all over the place. Someone has to have seen what happened to him—I'm sure of it. But no one will come forward."

"You think someone isn't telling the truth?"

"I just can't picture a scenario where *nobody* saw him. Those five minutes he was supposedly alone don't sit right with me. But it's hard to catch a ghost if they're not willing to say boo. If everyone's saying they didn't see him, that's what we have to work with. At least we know one person who came into contact with him before he disappeared."

"We do?" Olivia questioned. Kurt turned to Olivia as he walked, raising his eyebrows.

"I heard him and his ex-wife getting into it in the dressing room. About twenty minutes before he was due to go on stage, I went inside to check on my indoor security in the hall. I was crossing through this very hallway when I heard all the yelling and screaming. Man, was she mad."

Brock and Olivia traded a look. "What were they arguing about?" she asked.

"It was hard to tell … you know how it is when two people are yelling over the top of each other. It's impossible to get any sense out of it. But I think it was about the divorce. She kept shouting about how she'd been protecting him for so long—how he'd broken his promise to her. The gist of it was that he never asked her to do that, I think. So, of course, that made her even madder."

Poor Miranda, was Olivia's first thought, but she had to push it aside. Miranda hadn't exactly lied to her, but she hadn't heard the full truth from her mouth at the party. Knowing that she had been arguing with Landon a mere twenty minutes before his disappearance changed things. Especially now that she had her engagement ring in a plastic bag in her pocket.

"That didn't concern you?" Brock asked.

Kurt shrugged as he took them upstairs. "I wasn't trying to get in anyone's business, so I went on my way. You wouldn't believe the number of fights I hear in my line of work. By the time I walked back through, she had clearly left, and the dressing room was quiet. He was seen after that, so I don't know. Maybe she came back, but someone would've seen her, most likely. It wasn't on the cameras."

Olivia was torn. She still felt sure that Miranda had told her the truth the previous night. She was too drunk to do much else. But she had omitted some important details, and now that Olivia was aware of them, she didn't know what to think. It wasn't a good look for Miranda, that was for sure. Miranda would have to hold her breath and hope that no one found out that she'd been on the scene that night, or the tabloids would be all over her. That was the last thing she needed.

They made it to the security office, and Kurt unlocked it for them, allowing them in. There were a number of screens displaying the layout of the cameras in the building, and Kurt immediately sat down in front of them to gather the footage from the event.

"Believe me, I've sat down and looked through these videos a dozen times," Kurt told them. "I was worried I had missed something ... but I don't think I have. Here you can see the footage of the locked room where the envelopes were kept ... you can see the ushers guarding it like their lives depend on it, and with good reason. They're paid a lot of money for a simple job. But the video feed shows that the envelopes weren't tampered with, and no one touched them aside from the ushers and Sammy Rosehurst when he went on stage. So, I don't know how on earth someone managed to replace the message inside the envelope. And here you can see the footage from everywhere else in the building ... I spotted Landon a few times on the tapes, but those five crucial minutes, I didn't see anything out of the ordinary."

"Would you mind letting us look through it?" Brock asked.

"Sure. Maybe you'll spot something I didn't ... but it's hard to know what to look for when you don't know what happened to him. He's not seen leaving of his own accord, and he's not seen with anyone else. It's a conundrum."

"Did his dressing room have camera footage?" Olivia asked.

Kurt shook his head. "No. We don't have cameras in the dressing rooms for the privacy of the actors who use them. I'll bet that changes now though."

"It's a little late for that," Brock pointed out. "Do you mind if we sit here for a while and review everything? We want to make sure nothing has been missed."

Kurt sighed. "I don't see why not. But if you don't find anything, would you mind telling my boss that? If the freaking FBI can't find anything suspicious, then I can't have failed at my job, right?"

"We'll cross that bridge when we come to it," Olivia promised. Kurt did seem like he had been fairly well prepared for the night of the event. No one could've predicted that Landon Brown would go missing that night. But Olivia couldn't help thinking about the gaps in Kurt's plan. Was it possible that someone used those gaps to their advantage to smuggle Landon out?

After Kurt had left, Brock and Olivia spent the next few hours trawling through footage and discussing how someone might have managed to get Landon out without being spotted.

"If someone managed to disable him and carry him out, they must be strong," Olivia mused. "We're likely looking for a man who would be able to get him out of there with ease. But also somebody who knew the building well and knew how to get them both out of there without being spotted. Which means someone with knowledge of the blind spots that can't be seen by cameras."

"You think it might be someone from security?"

"Probably not. Like Kurt said, they were placed outside for most of the event. Someone would've seen them leaving their post, and they wouldn't have had time to return. No, I think it would have to be someone with less of an obvious role. Someone no one was keeping an eye on."

"Well, that could be anyone. It seems like no one saw anyone on that night. Unless someone is keeping very quiet about what they saw."

"Perhaps," Olivia said. "I think we're going to have to play the long game with this one. Kurt's right, there's very little to go on here. I'll ask for a copy of the tapes anyway so we can watch them back if we need to. But I think for this, we're going to need to think more outside the box. First, though, let's try to track down the ushers who had the envelopes and talk to them. I want to know their perspective on it all."

CHAPTER THIRTEEN

"I'VE TOLD EVERYONE THE SAME THING. I DIDN'T MESS UP anything with the envelopes."

Olivia and Brock were sitting opposite Dina Vasquez in her home in Inglewood. She was close to tears, biting her lip to stop them from falling. Olivia and Brock had managed to track her down through Kurt, but they had been informed before they arrived that Dina had been fired before the awards show had even ended.

"Something went wrong somewhere," Olivia said gently. "We know that because the envelope had the threatening message inside. We're not blaming you."

"Why not? Everyone else sure is," Dina snapped, her face creased with anxiety. "Five years I've been in this job, and I've never made a mistake once. Which is more than some awards shows can say. I've always done a good job. And now, just like that, I'm out of a job. And it wasn't my fault."

"Do you have an explanation for what you think happened?" Brock asked. "Because something went wrong somewhere. Any theories on what could've gone down?"

Dina threw her hands up in frustration. "I don't know, okay? That's the worst part of all this. I know that it wasn't me that was the problem, but I don't know where else to lay the blame. I stood there the entire day with those envelopes. No one else entered that room except for me, and I didn't leave it. The room was locked from the inside, by me. I stood guard like a dog all day. So, either someone interfered before I got there for the day, or they interfered after the handover. But it doesn't matter now. I'm out of a job."

"It matters," Olivia insisted. "Because if you've been framed for this, then we can help. We can probably help you get your job back if we can prove what happened with the envelopes. That's why we're asking. We trust what you're telling us, but we're going to need a bit more information."

Dina let out a long, deep sigh. "If had any to give you, I would. But I don't know what to say. I did everything I was supposed to and nothing more, nothing less. Believe me, I've been searching my mind for where I could've gone wrong ever since they let me go. I've barely slept; I've barely eaten. Do you know how it feels to be accused of failing? A man is missing, and my bosses seem to think that I delivered a threatening note on purpose to reveal his disappearance. What am I supposed to do with that information?"

Olivia didn't know what to say or how to comfort Dina. Everything she was saying made logical sense. But there was a missing link in the case—something that would connect the testimonies of everyone they'd spoken to. It was frustrating that they didn't know what that link was, but they'd find it… in time.

Olivia wanted Kurt and Dina to have their job security back. It made her angry that they were being threatened with layoffs and reprimands when they had clearly done nothing wrong. It seemed that though they worked with celebrities, they certainly weren't treated with the same grace as they were.

"Did anything look strange about the envelopes?" Olivia pushed, grasping at straws. "Did it seem like any of them had been tampered with, were the wrong color from the others, maybe had been opened before?"

"No," Dina said, cutting Olivia off before she'd even finished speaking. "None of that. Look, I've told you what I know. You're rubbing salt in the wound of me losing everything. I wish you luck with your investigation, but I don't want any part in it. You can call me when you get to the bottom of it and get me my job back."

Olivia sighed, but she didn't want to push more. Dina had clearly exhausted every piece of information she knew. There wasn't much else to say, and their attention would be better spent elsewhere.

"Thank you for your time, Dina. If you think of anything else, please call us. And maybe don't mention to anyone else that we were here. We're trying to run a quiet operation."

Dina snorted. "Of course, you are. Because God forbid the disappearance of some big shot make it to front page news. Will they talk about what this case is doing to ordinary people when word gets out? The ordinary people getting laid off because some asshole has gone missing? Of course, they won't. We'll be forgotten, as always."

"Dina…"

"I'm done with the conversation now. You can see yourselves out."

Olivia and Brock stood to leave. Olivia felt almost like a child being reprimanded. But she hated the fact that Dina was right. They still had no evidence that Landon hadn't just walked away on his own accord. And if he did, if he was just playing some elaborate prank, then did he consider who he was trampling on along the way? Probably not. It was true—ordinary people always ended up in the worst scenarios. The rich could buy their way out of almost anything.

But normal people couldn't afford that luxury.

It was getting late. The sun had set in the sky, and Olivia knew that they were done for the day. They'd gotten a lot done, and yet she felt they had shifted very little in their investigation. Olivia and Brock called Yara, and her driver came to pick them up. They didn't plan on spending another night at her home, but they needed to go and collect their belongings to take to their hotel. Olivia had told Brock they could stay with Yara if he preferred, but he shook his head at the suggestion.

"I don't feel comfortable at her house," Brock admitted. "I feel that we're standing in her way. Besides, I don't think she should be too involved in what we're doing. She knows more than she should, and if there is any danger in this case, I want to keep her safe."

"Of course."

"Do you think… do you think she'll be okay with us going elsewhere? I get the feeling she wants us around. Like she might be… lonely."

Olivia chewed her lip. They both knew something was off with Yara. Olivia barely knew her, but she could tell that she wasn't at her best. But what could they do? They were there to solve a case, not to babysit Yara Montague. Olivia reached for Brock's hand.

"It's not our job to take care of her," Olivia said. Brock frowned and pulled his hand away from hers. Olivia realized how her words had sounded and fumbled to replace them.

"Sorry. That's not what I meant. It's just that we're here for another reason. This isn't a social visit. I'm not saying you shouldn't reach out and see if she's okay…"

"You just think we have other priorities?" Brock said. There was pain in his voice, and Olivia knew she'd messed up. After all the times Brock had been there for her when she was worried about something or someone in her life, the least she could do was return the favor. She reached out for him again.

"I'm sorry. I was wrong. You're right. Yara is important. But she's a grown woman. She's been living alone long before we got here. And remember… we're having dinner with her tonight. We're not abandoning her, I promise."

Brock soaked in her words and then nodded. "Okay. I just…
I don't want to leave her the way she is. She seems so fragile. And
I'd never forgive myself if we walked away from her when she
needed someone the most."

"I understand," Olivia said with a nod. "We'll take the hotel,
but if she needs you, you go to her. I wouldn't ever stand in the
way of what you have together. You're a good friend to her, and I
love that about you. You don't need to change that."

Brock finally raised a small smile. "Sorry if I'm cranky. This
just feels like… a lot."

"It does. But it's alright. We're going to solve this one, just like
all the others. And when it's done… you take all the time you
need to help Yara out."

Brock reached out for Olivia's hand once more and entwined
their fingers. "Thank you," he murmured. Olivia squeezed
his hand.

"Don't mention it," she said as they pulled up at Yara's home.
"Now let's get dinner sorted out. Nothing cheers you up more
than a good meal."

CHAPTER
FOURTEEN

DINNER WAS NOT AS OLIVIA WAS EXPECTING, BUT IT WAS exactly what she should have been expecting. They arrived at Yara's home just after five o'clock and found her drinking more rosé in front of her TV, laughing loudly along with the canned laughter from the show she was watching. She let out a whoop when she saw that they had returned and threw her arms around both of them in an enthusiastic hug.

"Thank God you're back. I thought you had forgotten about our dinner plans! And our reservation is at seven! You need to get dressed, to look your best..."

"I thought we opted for a quiet night in?" Brock said warily, trying for a smile. Yara laughed.

"You're in Hollywood, Brock! There's no such thing as a quiet night in. And there's no chance I'm letting you leave this city without having a proper night out on the town."

"You know we can't really go drinking..."

"Just dinner and a couple of cocktails then! And then I promise I'll leave you be to get on with your work. Come on Brock, please? I barely ever get to see you. I just want to show you around the city. The place we're going to is simply *gorgeous*. Plus, if you simply can't switch off, there'll be tons of people to eavesdrop on for work. That's a good thing, right? And I *know* you want to sample the food..."

Brock wavered, glancing at Olivia. She knew he wanted her to chime in and give her opinion, but she had to leave this one up to him. Yara was his friend, and it was his decision how he chose to support her. She wasn't sure going out was a good idea, but she also imagined that swaying Yara from it would be more difficult than they could handle. Brock sighed, raking a hand through his hair.

"Alright, I think we can manage that..."

Yara clapped her hands together in delight. Olivia wondered how much she had drunk in their absence. It seemed like it must be quite a lot. "Wonderful. Olivia, why don't you pick something from my wardrobe? Brock, I'm sure you can outfit repeat just this once... you can head back to your hotel and get ready. Then meet me at *Célèbre* for dinner. Alright?"

They didn't have much choice but to agree. Yara spent the next fifteen minutes trying to get Olivia to try on everything in her wardrobe, but she quickly grabbed the first thing she could find and retreated to the car that was waiting for them outside. In their hotel, as they prepared for dinner, Olivia had a bad feeling in the pit of her stomach about Yara.

"Help zip me up?" Olivia asked Brock as she stepped into an elegant crimson dress that hugged her body. Brock did as she asked, his fingers lingering a while on the skin of her back, distracting her from her thoughts of Yara. But when he kissed her jawline gently, she returned to the present moment.

"Thanks for doing this," he told her. "I know it's probably not the best idea … but I didn't want to say no to her—didn't want to upset her unnecessarily."

"I know. It's okay," Olivia said. She wondered whether Yara was likely to make a scene while they were out. The last thing they needed was to draw attention to themselves and end up in the news. She could practically read the headline: *Yara Montague Has Public Breakdown After Visit From FBI.* She knew she was probably being overly paranoid, but they couldn't afford to blow the case. It was bad enough that Grayson Worth had their identities pinned and that they'd had to reveal themselves to the workers at the venue. If anyone figured out who they were, it would make investigating ten times harder.

"Are you ready?" Brock asked as Olivia quickly slicked on some red lipstick. She knew she had to make some effort if she was going to get into a swanky restaurant. She turned to Brock.

"Do you think I look ready?"

He smiled, his eyes drifting over her body. "You look perfect. I wish we could stay here instead of going to dinner."

Olivia blushed. "Yara is going to really appreciate this, I'm sure. And hey… you haven't had much of a chance to catch up yet. Maybe this will be the perfect time to talk properly."

Brock nodded. "You're right. This won't necessarily be a nightmare. It might even be fun. Shall we?"

Olivia felt very out of place as they walked through the lobby of their cheap hotel, dressed to the nines. It was also strange hailing down a cab when they clearly looked like the kind of people who had private cars to drive them around. The driver didn't even know where *Célèbre* was, so he had to search for it on his phone. He chuckled to himself as he drove them.

"Don't get many fancy people in my cabs. Not even in LA," he told them.

"Oh, we're not fancy at all. If I had my way, I'd be headed to a burger joint right now," Brock said with a smile. "We're just meeting a friend."

"Well, this place looks pretty fancy to me. Let's hope this friend doesn't expect you to split the bill, eh?"

It was just before seven when they arrived outside the restaurant. It was clear right away that the place was not for ordinary folk. There were bouncers outside, and the entrance was cordoned off by gold pillars and red rope. Olivia knew there was no way they were getting inside without Yara's reservation, but she was nowhere to be seen. They stood there waiting for what felt like an hour but was really only a few minutes. Olivia wrapped her arms around herself, fending off the chill that threatened to crawl on her skin.

"Where is she? She said she'd meet us at seven," Olivia said, glancing around her. Brock chewed his lip.

"It's only ten minutes past. You can imagine how traffic is."

But it was another ten minutes before Yara showed up, her car trundling down the road. Olivia raised an eyebrow at Brock. How did a woman with nothing but time on her hands manage to be late for dinner? Olivia had no clue. Still, she was glad to see Yara arrive, even if she did wince as she stumbled a little on her seven-inch heels.

"Who's hungry?" she crowed with a grin, like she wasn't nearly half an hour late to meet them.

"Are you sure they will have held our table?" Brock asked pointedly. "This place seems in high demand."

"Don't you worry about that," Yara brushed him off. "Everything will be fine. Let's go! I'm dying for a martini."

Olivia and Brock exchanged a look. *This is going to be a long night,* Olivia thought.

Sure enough, though, when they got inside, their table was still reserved. They were taken up a grand staircase to the dining hall where soft music was playing and rich diners were talking in quiet voices. Olivia knew right away that Yara would stick out like a sore thumb there. She didn't seem to have an indoor voice, and she was already pretty drunk. Olivia held her breath as they were led to their table, glad that the diners were at least spread far apart and the lighting was low. She hoped it would keep the attention away from them.

The entire menu was in French, so Brock happily translated for them, which distracted Yara for a little while. However, it wasn't long before Yara was ordering drinks for them all, which made Olivia's stomach twist.

"A round of martinis, a round of whiskey, and the most expensive bottle of bubbly that you have," Yara declared. Olivia shifted in her seat.

"That's really not necessary…"

"Of course, it is! You're my guests here, and I want you to have the best," Yara said. In the end, it was easier just to keep her appeased, so they quietly ordered their meals and let Yara jabber away at them without saying a word. They listened as patiently as they could, but Olivia could see that Brock was struggling to keep up with what she was saying. In their soberness, she wasn't making a lot of sense.

"You're both so quiet!" Yara laughed loudly, earning a snooty glance from a woman at a nearby table. Olivia swallowed, clenching her hand in her lap to stave off the anxiety. She wished they'd never agreed to go out. It was becoming clearer by the minute that Yara wasn't in a good place. The champagne arrived, and she made a noise of appreciation.

"Chef's kiss!" she said, kissing her fingers. The waiter offered her a polite smile before backing away as fast as he could. Yara seemingly had no idea that the people around her were judging her and wishing she would quiet down.

"What was I talking about?" Yara asked, cocking her head to the side. Brock smiled uncomfortably.

"I've totally forgotten."

Yara shrugged. "Ah, well. Can't have been very important then. Right! Let's raise a glass! To old friends, and to new. To happiness and to success. Those are good things to toast, right?"

"Yeah, definitely," Olivia said, smiling at Yara. She raised her glass at the same time as Yara, but Yara moved with significantly more force, smashing her glass against hers. It shattered, and Yara yelped loudly, broken glass and wine spilling on the table. Everyone was looking at them, and Olivia's heart seized. This wasn't good.

"Oh," Yara said in shock, suddenly appearing to be close to tears. "What have I done?"

A waiter came over to assist them, ushering them away from the table and insisting that they sit somewhere else. They were ushered to a private dining area with fewer tables. Olivia thanked the waiter while Brock helped Yara into her new seat, both of them trying to ignore the silent tears dribbling down her face. Her makeup was a little smudged, and she was hiding behind one of her hands, as if no one would be able to see her. Brock nudged her with his knee.

"Hey now, cheer up. It's only a broken glass... it could happen to anyone."

"But it happened to *me*," Yara said with a sniff. "These things always happen to *me*. I'm a disaster."

"No... don't say that," Olivia said gently. Yara gently dabbed at her eyes with a napkin.

"It's true. I know you must think I'm awful. I just... I like to drink and have fun. But sometimes I wonder if... if maybe it's not so fun anymore."

There was silence at the table. The elephant in the room was looming large over their table. Olivia wanted to give Yara a hug, but it was Brock that reached out to her, putting a hand on her shoulder. She looked up at him with tearful eyes, looking like a scolded child.

"Yara... you don't need us to tell you what you already know," Brock said. "You're drinking too much. Drinking during the day... it's not good. It has to stop. You can't keep doing this to yourself."

"I know," she whispered. "But... it's so hard to stop."

Olivia's heart sank. She knew how addiction could ruin lives, turn them completely upside down. And now she saw it eating away at Yara from the inside.

"You must think it's ridiculous," Yara sniffed, looking away from them both. "I've got the world in the palm of my hand, and I'm choosing to destroy everything I have built."

"It's not your fault," Olivia said gently. "Bad things happen to everyone. Addiction doesn't discriminate." She felt guilty now for how she'd judged the people she had come across. She knew that they had issues of their own, issues that all the money in the world couldn't easily solve. She'd been narrow-minded. Not all of them were egocentric, money-making monsters. Some were, but who was she to judge other people's flaws? She knew she had plenty of her own.

It was what made her human.

Yara had her head in her hands now. "I'm sorry. I hope I haven't embarrassed you both."

"Don't be ridiculous," Brock said soothingly. "Besides, you're the only person here who knows about my worst drunk incident, and we both know it's a lot worse than what happened here today."

Yara raised her head from her hands with a meek smile. "Am I allowed to tell Olivia to make myself feel better?"

He grimaced, but then grinned. "I'll allow it. So long as we ask the waiter to take away the bottle when he comes back. And then later, sometime this week… we'll talk more about this, okay? Let's try and enjoy this dinner, get some food to line your stomach… and then we can revisit this conversation when you're more clearheaded."

Yara's lip wobbled a little. "You're being so kind to me."

"Of course, we are. We're your friends," Brock insisted warmly. "We're not going to leave you out in the cold."

Yara took a deep breath and raised a smile. "Okay."

"Okay, good."

"I'm just going to visit the bathroom. Clean myself up a little," Yara said, standing a little unsteadily. "Thank you. To both of you."

As she retreated from the table, Olivia watched Brock breathe a visible sigh of relief. He caught her eye, looking exhausted. Olivia reached for his hand.

"You did well. You handled that perfectly."

"Do you think?"

"Definitely. I'm sure she really appreciates the way you spoke to her. And I'm proud of the way you dealt with it. That can't have been easy."

Brock's shoulders seemed to sag with relief. "What a night."

Olivia chuckled softly. "Yeah. It's been an interesting one."

"I'm glad you were with me for it. And I'm glad we might be able to help her."

Olivia smiled gently. "Me too. And for what it's worth... I like her. She seems like a lovely woman. And I never thought I'd say that about one of your exes."

Brock laughed. "I think she likes you too. She's taken a liking to you; I can tell. And I just hope you get to see her at her best while you're here. When she's not so... you know."

It was at that moment that Yara came running back from the bathroom, her eyes wide. Olivia was on her feet immediately, taking in the shock on Yara's face. She was worried that something bad might've happened.

"What is it?" she asked urgently. "Is everything okay?"

"You'll need to know this," Yara said in a loud whisper, slipping back into her seat and presenting her phone to them both. "News just in."

Olivia and Brock peered at the screen. There was a photograph of Miranda Morgan being bundled into her car by her security team, surrounded by eager paparazzi. Above it was the title of the article.

Miranda Morgan Stands to Inherit *Millions* if Landon Brown is Found Dead.

Olivia's stomach twisted when she saw the byline.

"Grayson Worth," she growled. "What has he found out? And how?"

"Landon never changed his will after their divorce proceedings," Yara said a little breathlessly. "So, if he's dead, then she's going to inherit everything of his. She may as well still be his wife. She's going to be *rich* rich."

Brock turned to Olivia. "This isn't looking good for her. With everything else we know so far... the argument, the ring, the *abuse*... "

Yara's eyes widened at the new information, but Olivia shot her a look that made her keep quiet. She was sober enough to understand that this was important.

"I know. It looks bad," Olivia said. "We're going to need to speak to her again. Maybe get a warrant for her home if she's uncooperative. Right now, all eyes are going to be on her. We wait until morning and see how things pan out. We don't want a bunch of paparazzi to inundate us at the gates to her home."

"I could arrange a meeting," Yara said, keeping her voice low. "I can let her know that I have a contact who can help her if she's willing. You can meet her somewhere off-grid and find out what her side of the story is."

"Thank you, Yara," Brock said. "That would be a big help."

Yara smiled to herself, looking pleased. At that moment, the waiter returned with their food, presenting it with a flourish. Food was the last thing on Olivia's mind ... until she saw how delectable it looked. She could see Brock's eyes lighting up too.

"We can put this conversation on hold," he said, eyeing the plate that was placed in front of him. "Tomorrow, we'll sort it out. Tonight ... let's enjoy ourselves."

CHAPTER FIFTEEN

D INNER WASN'T SO BAD CONSIDERING HOW IT HAD BEGUN. Olivia found that as Yara sobered up a little, she was very good company, and she had Olivia laughing until her sides hurt. It felt good to connect with someone from Brock's life. He was a private man, and he didn't have a lot of people that he considered worthy of being a part of their new life together, so getting to know Yara was a rare treat. She told Olivia stories of Brock as a younger man, things that Brock would be too shy to tell her about himself. As they left dinner that night, she felt like she not only knew Yara better, but Brock too.

"Are you going to be okay going home?" Brock asked as Yara's driver came to pick her up. "You've had a rough night. If you need some company…"

Yara waved him off with a smile that didn't quite reach her eyes. "Ah, I'm alright. I think the things we talked about… well, they've been on my mind for a while. I guess I just need to sit with my thoughts for a while."

"Well… if you need anything, call us," Olivia said gently. "If you need someone to talk to."

Yara shifted a little uncomfortably. Olivia wondered if this was the most sober she had been in some time. "I will… just not tonight. Tonight I just have some stuff to figure out." Olivia and Brock watched as she left, their hearts heavy in their chests. Olivia reached for Brock's hand, and he brushed his thumb over her knuckle.

"She'll be okay. She's one of the toughest people I know," Brock said, kissing the top of her head. "Second only to you. Let's get back to the hotel. After the article Grayson posted, I bet there's information all over the internet for us to dig into…"

They hailed a taxi and made it back to the hotel just before midnight. Yara had promised that she'd set up a meeting with Miranda for them the following day, but there was plenty to be done in the meantime.

"What do you think of it all?" Brock asked as they changed out of their dinner clothes. "You've met her. Do you think Miranda would kill Landon for the money?"

"Based on my impression of her? No, I don't believe for a second that she would. She was… fragile. That's how I'd describe her. The way Yara was tonight… she wasn't aggressive in her intoxication… she was broken. She was pouring her heart out to me. And though I'm sure the abuse she endured made her angry, I think more than anything, it made her sad. I think she lost the person she loved most, and I think she still cares deeply for him. I think it would be far from her nature to make something bad happen to him, let alone kill him."

"So, you think the inheritance is unrelated?"

"We have no indication that Landon is dead. And if he were, she wouldn't inherit the money if she killed him. I can't deny that something weird is going on, but right now, it feels hard to pin anything on anyone. We've got nothing to back up our claims except domestic speculation. Plenty of people go through messy divorces and don't try to off their ex."

"Most of them don't have millions of dollars at their expense to pay someone to do it either."

"That's true. But I just don't see it with Miranda. I have no idea what she'll be like sober though. She was pretty wasted when I met her. I wonder if she even remembers me."

"Hopefully she does. If she remembers how you treated her, she might be more willing to talk. I still think she's going to be pretty tight-lipped about the whole thing though. I would be, especially considering she's got a huge court case going on. If Landon returns, she still has that to go back to. If anything she says against him gets out, it might be considered defamation."

"We'll be discreet. Unlike Grayson Worth, we're not in the business of throwing everyone we meet under the bus," Olivia said bitterly. "I can't believe he wrote that article. What does he stand to gain? Do you think it's because he had a past connection with Landon?"

"Who knows what men like Grayson Worth are thinking? What I really want to know is how he got the information. He's giving us a run for our money. The FBI will be wanting to train him up."

"Don't even joke. The last thing we need is someone like him on our team. Still, it might be worth giving him a call. If we can offer him something small and insignificant about the case, maybe he'll give us something in return."

"Don't count on it. The only person he's trying to help is himself."

Olivia sighed. "You're not wrong. Well, what should we do now?"

"We can look into the article a little more. But I think it's best we get a good night's sleep to be ready for our interview with Miranda tomorrow. I have a feeling she'll have an interesting story to tell."

"Probably. And she might want that million-dollar ring of hers back too…"

Olivia and Brock stayed up reading the article that Grayson had published. They found no indication of where he'd got his information from, claiming in the article to have an anonymous source. When they found little else of interest, they gave in and headed to bed, sleeping off the day's worries until morning.

The sound of Brock's phone was what woke Olivia the next morning. As he answered the call, she checked her watch. It was almost nine a.m. *I'm getting too used to the LA lifestyle,* she thought as she forced herself to get up and take a quick shower.

When she returned from the bathroom, Brock was off the phone. Olivia dressed quickly, waiting for him to tell her what it was about.

"That was Yara. She's feeling a little worse for wear today, as you might imagine. I think this hangover has been chasing her for quite some time," Brock said, shaking his head sadly. "She said she was going to a spa today for some kind of detox treatment, but she's already put in a call with Miranda. She explained to her that we can help her, so she's agreed to meet us. But not until this evening. Miranda's home is swarmed with paparazzi. She's giving herself time to find a way out without being spotted."

"Well, good luck to her. If those paparazzi are anything like Grayson Worth..." Olivia shuddered.

"Well, I suppose that's her problem to deal with. Yara's going to send us the address where Miranda would like to meet. But that's not all we've got in the meantime."

"Oh?"

"Looks like Yara's had a very busy morning making connections for us. Apparently, Sebastian reached out... he apologized for the way he spoke to her the other day and for how he reacted to our questioning. They talked for a while, and he asked if he could trust us. She obviously vouched for us. Now, he wants us to revisit him at his home. He says he wants to talk to us instead of us barging in with a search warrant."

"Hmm. So, I'm guessing he has something at the house he doesn't want us to see?" Olivia raised an eyebrow. Brock wavered.

"Well... Yara told me to go easy on him. Apparently, he's told her why he was so cagey the other day. She's leaving it to him to explain, but she says everything makes sense now. He must have told her something interesting."

"Well, consider me intrigued. What time is he expecting us?"

"I said we'd go right away, and he said he'd send a car for us. I don't think taxis are allowed through where he lives. This has got to be important, right? I don't want to miss our chance to get ahead of the game. And who knows? Maybe we'll even beat Grayson to this information."

The car arrived for them ten minutes later, and Olivia spent the car ride wondering what Sebastian might want to talk to them about. He had been so determined not to talk the first time around, spooked from the moment Olivia brought up the meeting between Landon and Frank. So, what was he suddenly so open about?

He was waiting for them at the door again, but this time, he was dressed well in a shirt and dress pants. Olivia wasn't sure why he was so formal, but he even offered to shake their hands as they approached.

"Thank you for coming. Come inside…"

They followed him back to the living area they'd visited last time. There was a pot of tea on the coffee table, but no one reached for a cup. Brock and Olivia sat down, but Sebastian remained standing, even pacing back and forth a few times. He was anxious, and Olivia wanted to know why. What made Sebastian Morales tick?

"In your own time," Olivia said with a nod in his direction. Sebastian stopped pacing and took a deep breath, smoothing down his shirt. He was visibly sweating from his armpits.

"The first thing I need you to know is… is that I am only telling you this because I want to clear my name. If this information is released, if it makes its way out of this room, I *will* be pressing charges. Is that clear?"

"That depends on what you're about to tell us," Brock countered. "Did you have something to do with the disappearance of Landon Brown?"

"No."

"Have you done something illegal?"

"No."

"Then you're fine."

"You promise?" Sebastian pressed.

"We won't give up your secret, Mr. Morales," Olivia said. "Can you please just tell us why we're here?"

Sebastian let out a lungful of air, looking like he was visibly deflating. "There has been much speculation about my connection to Landon in the past year… it is well-known by the public that we apparently don't get along. But it's not true. It's a story we've had to concoct to explain things in the media. It helped keep prying eyes away from the nature of our relationship."

"What are you saying?" Olivia asked.

He sighed. "I'm saying… Landon is my boyfriend."

Olivia raised an eyebrow. Now that wasn't what she'd been expecting to hear. She leaned forward, ready to listen to what Sebastian had to say. He calmed himself with a deep breath, avoiding their eye contact.

"Landon and I met on the set of *Starless Night,* but I have admired him from afar for a long time. And when he admitted his feelings for me, I told him that I felt the same. But it was complicated. My family is very… traditional. To be seen with a man would make my life very difficult. And at the time, Landon was still married to Miranda. We knew that our only option was to keep our relationship a secret, so that's what we did. We ensured there was no way for anyone to trace our courtship back to either one of us. We went on fake dates with women. We gave the paparazzi the story they wanted—the story they expected… and of course, we are actors. So, we used that to our advantage. I would like to believe we have put on a convincing show."

"You certainly have," Brock said, sounding almost impressed by the revelation. "And you're telling me that nobody outside this room, other than Landon, knows about this?"

Sebastian wavered. "There are others who know. Miranda found out, after a while."

"She caught you?" Olivia asked.

"No. I refused to be with Landon properly until we told her. It wasn't fair for her to be trapped in a loveless marriage. Things were already bad between them, but Miranda was a friend of mine. I refused to be the other man in the relationship, and I refused to let Landon cheat for me. I crossed many lines during my time with Landon ... but if Miranda hadn't agreed to end things quietly with Landon, I would have left him."

"And how is your relationship with Miranda, following everything that happened between the three of you?"

Sebastian chewed his lip. "It is complicated. We still care for each other. I have nothing against her. But as you can imagine ... she feels a little betrayed by me. And that's okay. How couldn't she feel that way? However, Miranda has been very good to us— better than she had to be. She promised to keep our secrets and to go along with the ruse."

"Are you aware of what has been said about her in the news?"

Sebastian nodded. "Yes. But Landon didn't simply forget to change his will. He planned to amend it, but he wasn't going to cut out Miranda entirely. Given everything he put her through, we all agreed that she should receive a share of the will. But I tried to stay out of their legal pursuits. The last I heard, Miranda was trying to get Landon to give her an immediate payout."

"Did it have anything to do with the court case?" Olivia asked.

Sebastian froze. He averted his gaze. "You know about the allegations she made against him?"

"We do."

Sebastian leaned against the arm of the sofa. "They were true. My partner isn't perfect. He did hit her once in a drunken state. I don't condone what he did. In fact, it was me who suggested that there should be a legal resolution to what he did. But it made things messy and complicated." He shook his head. "I know most people would tell me I'm crazy to stay with him ... he is a flawed man. I know that, and I know that he's done bad things. But behind closed doors, there is a reason he is the love of my life. He is a *good* person. He is charitable. He gives most of his money to good causes. He visits children in hospitals, attends charity events, has meet and greets with his fans. I know he's had his struggles. But he really is trying to improve, and I want to help him. He needs support." He paused, looking at Olivia with an imploring gaze.

"And that's why I'm telling you all of this. I need him found. I don't believe that he would ever just leave me without saying a word … I think someone made him disappear. And I'm scared for him."

"What was the last thing he said to you? Do you recall?"

Sebastian's eyes filled with tears, and he looked away. "He told me he loved me. On the phone, before the show. He was obviously drunk, which scared the hell out of me. The pressure of everything has been getting to him lately. The fame, the divorce, the secrets, the court case… but he said he loved me no matter what. That was… that was the first time he's said it out loud. I always knew he felt it, but he's never said it. Until then."

"You don't think that was his way of saying goodbye?" Brock pressed gently. "Because he intended to disappear?"

Sebastian shook his head, wiping at his eyes. "He wouldn't do that to me. He just wouldn't." He was choking up now. He looked at Olivia once again. "Please. That man is everything to me. Please promise you'll try to bring him back to me."

Olivia knew she could never make a promise she wasn't able to keep. She knew she had to be careful. But she looked back at Sebastian and saw the pain in his eyes. She imagined being in his shoes. When she had almost lost Brock, it tore her apart inside. She knew exactly how Sebastian was feeling.

"We're doing everything we can," Olivia said. "And if it's possible to find him, we will. I swear it."

CHAPTER SIXTEEN

"**F**EELS KIND OF WEIRD SITTING IN A DINER WITH A million-dollar ring in my pocket," Brock whispered to Olivia. She smiled. It certainly wasn't something she thought they would ever do—meeting one of the biggest stars in Hollywood. Olivia was anxious about seeing Miranda again, wondering whether she would recall their first meeting at all. She didn't want to make her feel uncomfortable, and she didn't want her to feel like she had only helped her for information. Yes, she didn't turn Miranda away when she started telling her everything she needed to know, but Olivia would never abandon a woman in need. She would've helped her regardless, and she didn't want Miranda to believe otherwise.

Miranda had chosen the location herself. It was a sweet little bistro tucked away in Brentwood that didn't have many customers. Apparently, she had used it before as a place to hide away from prying eyes. Olivia and Brock had been waiting almost an hour there, but Olivia was sure that it wasn't going to be easy for Miranda to get out of her home unnoticed, given the paparazzi gathered outside her home. She was willing to be patient if this got them the information they desperately needed.

Eventually, when Brock was onto his second cup of coffee, a woman walked in through the door. She was like a ghost of the Miranda Olivia had seen the other night. She was pale, not wearing makeup, her hair limp. A pair of large sunglasses were placed over her eyes, and she was dressed in dreary clothing. She certainly understood how to make herself disappear, to blend in to society despite her fame. She spoke quietly with the waiter, who pointed at Olivia and Brock's booth to direct Miranda. She walked over slowly, her face devoid of emotion as she slid onto the bench opposite Olivia and Brock.

"Thank you for meeting with me," she said stoically, taking off her glasses. Her eyes were ringed with dark circles. Clearly, she'd had a few sleepless nights. "I'm Miranda."

"I'm Olivia, and this is my partner Brock. I… I'm not sure if you remember…"

"I do, now that I see you here," Miranda said, eyeing Olivia anxiously. "You were sent to spy on me?"

"I assure that my intentions were good, Miranda. We were at the party to investigate Landon's disappearance. But I saw a woman in need and wanted to help. The rest…"

"It's alright. You didn't force me to spill my guts to a stranger," Miranda said with a bitter chuckle. "I don't recall everything I told you… but I suspect you already know much more about me than you should. So, I see no harm in telling you the rest."

"We're grateful for your cooperation," Brock said. "We know that your relationship with your ex-husband is… complicated."

Miranda sighed. "Yes, that does tend to be the way with divorce. I can't say Landon is my favorite person, but I do want him found. It's a tricky business hating someone you once loved.

Part of you wishes that terrible things would happen to them just so that they can feel the same way they made you feel. But another part of you wants them to get their happily ever after."

"You're a bigger person than I am," Brock remarked. "If I were in your shoes, I don't think I would have any positive thoughts left to give."

Miranda lowered her gaze to the table. "Landon was an endlessly charming man. I guess that some part of me is still under the spell he cast. I'd do anything to get him back safely. Even if he won't be returning to my side."

Olivia felt a pang of pity for her. Miranda was clearly having a hard time with everything. But Olivia had to remind herself that of everyone they'd interviewed so far, Miranda had the strongest motive to make something bad happen to her ex-husband. Not only had he cheated on her, gone through a messy divorce with her, and physically abused her, but he also got into a relationship with one of her close friends. Any one of those things alone would be enough to push anybody over the edge.

"We have something of yours," Olivia said quietly. Brock took the ring out of his pocket and slid it across the table. Miranda looked away from it, not taking it from the tabletop.

"We know you were in Landon's dressing room shortly before he disappeared," Brock said. "And we know that you argued. So, what we'd like to know is, why did you go there? And given that you argued pretty publicly with him, can you prove that you didn't do anything to make him disappear?"

Miranda didn't look shocked at the line of questioning. After a moment, she took the ring from the table and slid it into the pocket of her coat.

"I wanted to talk money," Miranda said plainly. "I'm not sure how much you know about my affairs already… but I was involved in a court case against Landon. He hit me once, and he wore me down mentally over the time we were together. His new… his new partner encouraged him to give me what I wanted, to get the mess over and done with. But Landon is a stubborn man. He can never just do things in a simple way. So, we were fighting endlessly in court. And recently, it's been starting to wear me down. I just wanted it all to be over. So, I went to him. I told him that if he was willing to end the court case and give me what I wanted, then he'd never have to hear from me again. Of course, our paths will naturally cross. We work in the same industry. But honestly... I'm tired. I don't want to keep doing this. I just want to move on with my life. I don't even care about the money; I've got plenty of that. It's just the principle. I wanted him to pay somehow for what he put me through... and in truth, I thought it would be easier to get money out of him than an apology."

Olivia's stomach twisted. *What a desperately sad thing to say,* she thought. She had been painting an image of Landon in her head over the past few days, and now all she could see was a monster. She couldn't help feeling sorry for Miranda. She still didn't know for sure what the woman was guilty of, if anything; but on some level, who could blame her if she did want to get rid of Landon? He'd made her life a living hell.

"You must think that I'm pathetic," Miranda went on with a sad smile. "But love does strange things to us all, doesn't it? I will always love Landon. I guess part of me went to the dressing room that day to have it out because I knew... I knew that would be the last time we came face to face like that. I knew he was going to give me what I wanted that day. And he did. He said he would give me the payout. He said he was done fighting too."

Miranda's eyes filled with tears. "And it hurt me. Because that was the moment I realized that there was no going back. We were done for good. I guess some part of me clung on, believing we might make it through. But resolving the money feud meant he was finished. So, I left with what I came for... but I think it gave me closure too."

"How much was the payout?" Brock asked bluntly. Miranda sniffed.

"Not really anything. Twenty million dollars."

Olivia could not stop her jaw from dropping open at that. "T—twenty *million*—" she sputtered, but Brock nudged her under the table, and she composed herself.

If Miranda was offended by Olivia's outburst, she didn't notice it. Instead, she gave a sympathetic smile, as if Olivia had agreed that it was a pittance. "I know. I could've pushed for more, I think… but I was satisfied. I brought with me some of my financial records for you to examine if you wish. Landon must have dropped a call to his lawyer letting him know that he had agreed to all of my terms. My money is in escrow, but I won't be keeping it. It's going to charity."

"But you're due for a much bigger payout if Landon doesn't return, aren't you?" Brock asked smoothly. "We spoke to Sebastian. We know that there were some discrepancies about Landon's will."

Miranda sighed. "The will was another issue, yes. I don't know how the hell Grayson Worth found out that information. He's been a thorn in my side for a long time. I think he and Landon had some kind of arrangement where he was paying him off. But I have no such deal, so I suppose he's happy to throw me under the bus. The will wasn't something that the three of us were concerned about. I mean, none of us expected it to matter yet… we're all young and in good health. I didn't think the will would matter. It was Sebastian who told Landon to keep me in the will. I think his guilt drove him to say that. He was so eager to stay on my good side, as if he didn't already take away everything from my life."

"Sebastian said you were friends."

"He was my friend. Until he wasn't. Still, I wasn't going to turn down an inheritance from Landon. I would spend his money better than he ever would. But we put that issue on the back burner because we had other things to consider. And now… well, I suppose it looks bad on me. Of course, the woman is always to blame. Not Landon for forgetting to change his will. Not Sebastian for complicating things. Me, the woman who just wanted to move on in peace. That will is a constant reminder of what I lost. Now the media is calling me a gold digger for something I have no control over."

Olivia nodded in understanding. She knew how the media typically twisted things to make the men of the world come out on top. They lived in a man's world, and Olivia had seen that come into play many times during her career. Women were blamed for how they spoke, how they acted, what they wore, who they associated with. And more often than not, they were the ones being abused, killed, assaulted. Olivia could see where Miranda's frustrations were coming from.

"There was a reason I kept everything private," Miranda continued. "I didn't want anyone to find out about the court case I had against Landon. I endured a lot in my marriage, and I understood that it would be used against me. If I called Hollywood's sweetheart an abuser, people would try to discredit me. They'd ask why I didn't speak up sooner? They'd call me a bitter old hag because Landon chose to move on, and I would be blamed for not letting it go. I understood all this and kept it to myself. I suffered alone through the trial because I knew that it would be so much harder with the world watching. And when he went missing… I knew people would be looking at me. I'm the scorned woman in the world's eyes. Why wouldn't I try to make the man who ruined me disappear? But life is more complicated than that. People assume they know us, understand us, because they saw us on a screen. But they don't know the real me, or the real Landon, or even Sebastian. What happened between the three of us should be our business alone. It has nothing to do with whatever happened to Landon."

Olivia wanted to be convinced. Everything she was saying made so much sense. But she couldn't discount her entirely. She still had motive, and she hadn't yet provided her alibi for the night of Landon's disappearance. Besides, Miranda was an actress. Had she been rehearsing these lines all day, preparing for the role she had to play? Olivia couldn't be certain of anything. Her gut was telling her to trust Miranda, but her mind was telling her to be more cautious.

"Can you tell us where you were when Landon disappeared? We believe he must have disappeared at some point just before eight o'clock. He was seen five minutes prior to going on stage, and then he missed his cue. Where were you at that point in time?"

"I was already in my seat by then. You can ask any number of people around me. I was sitting between Florence Marsh and Brit Carrow. After I left Landon's dressing room, I headed outside briefly to gather myself, but then I went straight there. I believe I sat down at around ten to eight."

Olivia was sure that someone would be able to confirm that alibi. Of course, there was no way of knowing if Miranda had simply paid someone to do her dirty work for her. But as Miranda slid a file across the table, she raised an eyebrow at Olivia.

"My financial records, as I mentioned," she said. "You can see all of my outgoings from each account. I assure you; I did not pay someone to get rid of Landon. But I understand you have to do your job. I'm happy to answer any other questions you might have, and I'll stick around in town for as long as you need me to. But as soon as this is resolved, I'm getting the hell out of here. I'm done with Hollywood. It's not everything it's made out to be."

Miranda left shortly after, and Olivia and Brock exchanged a look with one another.

"Thoughts?" Brock asked Olivia. She shook her head.

"I don't think she did this. She's been very forthcoming with us today... and the other night. I don't think she's the person we're looking for. But we should keep an eye on her all the same. Because if she was acting that whole time, she deserves a damn Oscar."

CHAPTER SEVENTEEN

I T WAS THE NEXT MORNING WHEN OLIVIA AND BROCK
secured the warrant to look inside Landon Brown's house.
Sebastian had agreed to meet them at the house to let them
in since he knew the codes for the various security gates. Since
Yara was on her spa retreat, she'd given the number of her
driver to use, and he willingly picked them up to take them to
the house. Olivia felt a little odd having a driver at their beck
and call. She missed how it was on their usual cases, where
she and Brock would drive around together, talking about
the nuances of the case. But this time, they were quiet as they
headed to Landon Brown's home.

Olivia could feel the magic of Hollywood slipping away from
her. She missed the simplicity of life in Belle Grove. Here, it was

like people lived under a different set of rules—rules to set them apart from ordinary folk. But to Olivia, it just seemed twice as tiring. All the games these people played with money and social standards—the way they used their power against other people to try to build their social standing—Olivia didn't understand how any of them could live that way.

Landon's house was by far the most lavish they'd come across. He clearly wasn't shy about flaunting his money, though the high walls around the house did keep him mostly safe from prying eyes. The building was a modern glass giant, with large panels allowing them to see everything in the house as soon as they made it through the gates. Sebastian met them at the front of the house, looking anxious to be there. Olivia wondered how they'd managed to carry on their secret affair for so long when Landon's house was like an invitation for everybody to see into his life.

"I never spent much time here," Sebastian muttered to Olivia, as if reading her mind. "This place is not much to my taste. Do you mind if I leave you to it? I have no desire to be caught lurking around here. The media would have a field day."

"Of course. Thank you for your help."

"Just make sure you lock everything up when you're done. And leave everything where it's supposed to be. Landon would kill me if he knew I'd let someone tamper with his things."

"Landon should be grateful that we're doing what we can to find him," Brock pointed out. Olivia could tell that he was getting irritated at being bossed around by rich people who didn't know how to be polite. Olivia understood that most stars saw people like them as chess pieces they could just move around and control without consequence. It was tiresome being in a world where they were considered second-class citizens.

Besides, they were searching for a man who clearly had a gray moral compass. They were looking for a cheat, an abuser, a drunk. Landon Brown was not a good man, no matter how the world saw him. It didn't mean they were working any less hard to find him, to find out what happened to him; but Olivia had to admit, this case felt different. She so often got invested in the victims and wanted to find them safe and sound. This time, she found she wasn't quite so eager to see him come back.

Not that she'd admit that out loud. She shook the thought off and approached the house. There was work to be done, and her personal thoughts on the man in question wouldn't slow her down. She was going to do her job well, as she always did. It wasn't her place to start judging, and a lot of people were counting on her to bring Landon home safely. That would be her driving force, if nothing else.

The house was eerily clean and untouched. It was as if no one really lived there. Olivia had to question how much time Landon really spent there. If Sebastian wasn't a common visitor there, it was likely they had a private residence where they would meet, or they spent more time in Sebastian's home. As opulent as it was, Sebastian's place did feel like a home; this place didn't.

"I guess we should just get to searching," Olivia started. "Look for any personal items, any communication devices… absence of things that aren't here, but should be."

"This place is huge," Brock said, pulling on a pair of plastic gloves. "It's going to take forever."

"Well, if forever is how long it takes, then we should get moving. Time spent standing around won't get us any closer to the finish line."

They split up and went in different directions, and Olivia began to navigate the maze of the house. Everywhere she went, she was surrounded by wide glass windows, and even though there was no one around, she had a prickle on her neck sensing she was being watched constantly. She tried to be sensitive to Landon's belongings as she rooted through them, but she soon found that Landon was a relatively minimalist man. He seemed to have very few personal items in this house that was almost more like a modern art museum than a house. It was so sparse that Olivia wondered whether Landon really had just packed up his things and moved away without telling anyone where he was going. It seemed like the kind of ridiculous, selfish behavior that a man like him might partake in.

Olivia was hoping for something—anything—that might help her out. She searched in the office for notebooks, for any scribblings Landon might have made, but came up with nothing. There was a calendar on his desk, but there was nothing written in it. Olivia checked his computer, too, but it was almost like it had never been used. It wasn't password protected, and there were no saved files on the computer. Landon had somehow lived in this place, but it was like he was walking through snow without leaving a footprint, no impression of himself on the place he called home.

It didn't actually take very long for Olivia and Brock to meet back somewhere in the middle, both of them unenthused by what they'd found.

"This place has weird vibes," Brock said to her as they looked around, hoping something new might materialize before their eyes. "He's got more money than most people will ever have, and yet he owns absolutely nothing…"

"I think it's supposed to be trendy. Minimalist living or whatever. I've heard stories of other big celebrities doing the same."

"Well, I think it's weird. If I was this rich, I'd at least buy a really big TV or something. What's the point? Everyone's so desperate to be a millionaire, but this guy was practically living in a warehouse."

Olivia shook her head. "I've stopped trying to make sense of any of it. Have we checked outside? There was a garage, right?"

"I think so… I guess we've got nothing better to do than look. This place seems like a total bust."

They headed back out the front of the house and to the garage. It took them a while to figure out how to get inside, but they found the control panel for the shutters inside the house. They watched the garage door lift up to reveal nothing but an empty space inside. Olivia frowned.

"Okay, I refuse to believe he didn't even own a car."

Brock shrugged. "I mean, Yara doesn't have one. I don't think she even has her license. Why would you need one if you have someone to drive you around everywhere?"

"Then why have a garage?" Olivia pointed out. "Well, we can quickly figure out what's going on here. We'll call Sebastian. He would know if he had a car. And if he does have one… where is it? Maybe that will explain some things."

Olivia called Sebastian's number, and he picked up almost right away.

"Hello? Are you finished already at the house?"

"Almost. We didn't find much of anything… but we just checked out the garage. There's no car there. Does he own a car at all?"

"Yes, he does. It's one of the few things he actually does own in his creepy little tomb house. The man has no taste… but his car is a thing of beauty. You're saying it's gone?"

"Yes. Which might be significant. Do you have the license plate? We can try to track it down if you know it."

"I can do you one better. The car has a GPS tracking feature. I have an app that connects it to my phone. We've used it the whole time we've been dating so that I know where to meet him without risking sending texts and making phone calls and getting caught. I'll check it now."

Olivia waited with baited breath while Sebastian searched for the GPS signal.

"Hmm," he said.

"What? Did you find something strange?"

"Sort of… the car is still parked at the diner where Landon met up with Frank on the day of the show. But I already knew that. I checked it a hundred times when he went missing. He must have called a car to bring him to the show and left it there. I was hoping… hoping he'd come back and pick it up, I guess."

"So, he can't have driven off anywhere then. Unless he used a different car," Olivia mused. "I think Brock and I will have to pay a visit to that diner. I don't know what went down between him and Frank at that meeting, but I'm curious to know. Perhaps we can get the staff to give us some insight. It might be one step closer to finding Landon."

"Well, if you think it'll help. Anything to bring Landon home. I'll send you the address."

Olivia ended the call with Sebastian and turned to Brock. "We're going to the diner where Frank and Landon met up. I think it's the next piece in the puzzle."

Brock grinned. "Well, I never say no to a trip to a diner. Lead the way."

CHAPTER
EIGHTEEN

T HE STARSTRUCK LOUNGE WAS A LITTLE OFF THE BEATEN
track, but it did appear to be a popular place to go. As
Olivia and Brock stepped inside, they saw that the walls
were covered completely with pictures of famous stars. Most
of the booths were filled, and Olivia was shocked to see a
few familiar faces from the silver screen sitting at the tables
and eating.

"Some place to stay out of sight," Olivia murmured. A peppy
hostess came over to greet them.

"Welcome to the Starstruck Lounge!" she declared. "And yes,
if you're wondering, you are among the stars here. Every single
picture on the wall is of a star who has visited here. People come
from far and wide to go stargazing."

Olivia glanced around her. Now she could see how it was the perfect location for Landon and Frank to meet up. Frank claimed they'd gone there to hide away from the world and to avoid being overheard in public, but it was obvious now that they were hoping to make a spectacle of themselves, to be seen together, to draw attention to their meeting. No wonder Frank had been shouting from the rooftops about it at the party. Olivia shook her head to herself. It was so typical, and she hadn't even seen it coming.

"Can I get you guys a table?" she asked, bringing Olivia back down to earth. She cleared her throat.

"Actually, we're not really here to eat. We're here investigating the disappearance of Landon Brown," Olivia told her in a low voice. The last thing they needed in a place like this was to have people looking their way. Unlike Landon and Frank, they really did intend to lie low. "We were wondering if we could talk to the staff who were working the day he came here? We've tracked his car to the parking lot here."

"So *that's* who that car belongs to," the hostess said with a shake of her head. "We were going to have it towed, but we didn't want to get sued by some big shot… and now I'm glad we didn't. Two of our waitresses were working that day that are here today. Come on back, I'll get them for you."

"That would be amazing. Thank you."

The waitress flashed them a winning smile and then sauntered off behind the bar to talk to some of the young girls on duty. A few looks were shot in Olivia and Brock's direction, then the two young girls headed over to collect Olivia and Brock.

"Hi," a young woman with auburn hair and a freckled face said to them. "I'm Poppy, and this is Becky," she said, nodding to a slim blonde girl beside her. "You can come with us around the back. We have a staff area where we can talk."

Olivia and Brock followed the girls through the kitchens and into a small room that had several diner booths.

"Can we get you anything before we talk?" Poppy asked, her tone a little wary. Olivia could understand that. No young person wanted to be interviewed by an authority figure. Brock opened his mouth, likely about to order a milkshake, but Olivia shook her head.

"We're fine, thank you. We won't keep you too long. We just want to talk about the day Landon Brown was here."

Becky blushed and giggled, and Poppy rolled her eyes ever so slightly. "He was a big hit with the staff," Poppy said pointedly. "We don't usually get *real* stars here. It's usually C-listers hoping to boost their profile, or some has-beens looking for a little attention. Celebrities that come here know they're going to be hassled for autographs and such. That's why people come here, to meet celebrities. It's certainly not for the food. But the day Landon was here… well, I guess it felt special."

"He's so handsome," Becky gushed with another giggle. "Even more than on TV."

"So we've heard," Olivia said diplomatically. "But what we're hoping to know is why he was here and what impression he made on you."

Poppy frowned. "I'm not sure what you mean."

"Well… did anything seem off about him? He disappeared later that day. And we've heard some reports that he was drunk on the red carpet. So was he… I don't know… was he being rude, or particularly loud, or acting strangely?"

"Drunk?" Becky frowned. She seemed to take the news personally. "But he's gone sober…"

"I'm just saying what I heard," Olivia said, raising her hands defensively. "Did you see anything like that?"

Poppy shook her head slowly. "No… he was perfectly polite. The man he was with… that director guy… he was kinda gross. He kept looking me up and down like a piece of meat. But I'm not really here for the celebrity experience. I'm here because people tip much better when they've just met a celebrity. Makes them feel rich."

"Landon was just *lovely,*" Becky chimed in, her eyes distant as she recalled the moment. "I got to serve him lemonade, and he called me *darling.* He said, 'Thanks, darling.'" She let out a wistful sigh. "I'll never forget the way he said it. It felt so *personal.* Like I was special."

Olivia didn't want to disappoint the girl by revealing that Landon likely wasn't interested in women at all, let alone some young fan who served him lemonade. She just smiled and nodded. "I'm sure that was very exciting. So, he was in a good mood? Did you hear anything that he and Frank talked about?"

Poppy shook her head. "I didn't. They tend to stop talking when you go over to serve them. And I think Becky was too starstruck to get much of anything."

"It was the best day of my life," Becky said dreamily. Olivia was starting to think that they should just interview Poppy alone. Becky didn't seem like she would be much use beyond gushing about mingling with the stars. Still, what could she expect from two girls who were barely brushing eighteen?

"I know it's not easy to remember details when you're not looking for them… but what about their body language? Did they seem to be having a positive conversation?" Olivia pushed. Poppy sighed, clearly getting bored of the line of questioning.

"I don't know. Not particularly? Honestly, it was too busy that day for me to pay too close attention. I guess a few people found out he was there and wanted to come and seek him out. I'm not sure how much talking they even got to do. There were a lot of fans hassling them during the meal."

"How long did they stay?"

"Maybe an hour. And at least half of that time was spent talking to fans. It seemed like they probably came to make an appearance rather than to actually talk."

Olivia pondered on that thought for a minute. Frank had said that they went there to talk things out, but that Landon hadn't had much interest in the matter. Was that why Landon suggested they go to the Starstruck Lounge? To avoid actually having to talk to Frank? It was a childish move, but it didn't mean it wasn't the one he made.

"Is there anything else you can think of that might be useful to us?" Brock asked. "I know you girls want Landon to come home safely. Anything you can tell us now will help us do that."

Poppy shrugged. "I'm sorry. I don't know what else to say. All I remember is that neither of them left a tip. Not even Frank after the way he eyed me up. Maybe I should've pandered to them more, given them the attention they wanted. Maybe then they would've filled up my college fund."

"I hope they come back again when Landon comes back," Becky added. "I'm only here until the end of this summer. I want to meet them again if I can."

"Yeah, that's the priority," Poppy mumbled, rolling her eyes. "I'm sorry we couldn't be of more use to you. I was too busy juggling my tables to pay more attention."

"That's alright, you've been a big help," said Olivia. "Do you mind going to grab your manager? We'd like to ask about the security cameras as well."

"Sure," Poppy nodded. "Wait here. I'll get my boss."

"That would be great, Poppy. Thank you so much," Brock said.

Poppy left, and Becky waved goodbye before she followed Poppy. A few minutes later, the hostess from earlier returned with a smile.

"Sorry to keep you waiting. We're swept off our feet today. I think since Landon Brown went missing, it's become even more of a novelty to come here. Good for business, I guess. Come on back, and I'll show you the footage."

They headed into a cupboard-sized room to look at the footage. The manager left them to their own devices, and they watched the footage closely on the two cameras. One of them was inside the diner, situated in the corner and covering almost the entire room. Olivia could just about make out Landon and Frank, but not their expressions. Then there was another camera for the parking lot, but it didn't quite capture all of the space outside. There were blind spots, which was frustrating.

"There's Landon's car," Olivia said, pointing it out. "But it obviously hasn't moved since then, and Landon never drove it again after going inside the diner… so what do we make of what we see?"

"Maybe we should keep an eye on the other cars," Brock said. "Perhaps we'll see something unusual."

They kept their eye on the parking lot, occasionally glancing at the footage of Landon and Frank inside, but there wasn't much to glean from the blurry images of them.

A few minutes into their time in the diner, another car appeared and parked on the left of Landon's car. Olivia watched, waiting for someone to get out of the car, but the doors never opened. Instead, the figure inside seemed to lean over and stare intently at Landon's car. She frowned. Why would someone just sit beside his car?

"Are you thinking what I'm thinking?" Brock asked, nodding to the car. Olivia nodded.

"A stalker, maybe. But it's strange that they haven't gone inside to see Landon, if that's who they're looking for. Do you think we should run the plate?"

"It can't hurt. I'll write it down."

While Brock was doing that, Olivia sped up the footage a little to see if anything of interest might happen. The car didn't budge, not even after Landon and Frank stood up from their booth and left the diner. Olivia set the speed back to normal on the footage, but Frank and Landon didn't appear in the footage. They must've been in the blind spots.

"I wonder where Landon went… I mean, he made it to the premiere later. Maybe he just got a lift with Frank?"

"Maybe," Brock said. "But they weren't exactly on good terms, from what we know. Would they really carpool together? And unless Landon was secretly drinking, I'm not sure why he'd bother leaving his car behind. It all seems odd to me."

"Well, he clearly left the diner somehow, because he's not showing up. But that car is still parked next to him… maybe he's waiting for him to come back too."

They continued to watch for a while. The car next to Landon's never budged, and the figure never got out. It had been sitting there for over an hour and a half when a new car showed up and parked on the other side of Landon's. Brock let out a chuckle.

"I don't think I'd be brave enough to park next to that car. I'd be scared of scratching it."

"Me too… but these people seem to have no problem with getting up close and personal, do they?"

They watched as a young woman got out of the car, glancing around herself. Then, she stuck her face up to the glass of Landon's car, peering inside as if she were looking for something.

Or someone.

"Why is she looking inside Landon's car?" Olivia mused.

"Maybe because it's the fanciest one in the lot."

"Maybe… but look at her. She parked right next to it, and she's really scouting it out. She obviously didn't steal it because it's still here… is it possible she knows who it belongs to? That she's looking for Landon?"

"I guess so. Maybe someone put on social media that they'd seen him at the diner? I suppose that's how people find out where to be and when. But did she really drop everything to come and find him?"

They watched as the young woman went out of the shot and headed inside the diner. She spoke to the waitress at the door, and then turned and headed back outside. She had her head in her hands, like she was crying, and she ran back to her car. She sat in it for a few minutes before driving off.

"Well, looks like she was here for Landon or Frank, definitely," Olivia said. "I think we need to look into this. Both cars."

"Agreed. And maybe it's time we paid Frank a visit too. He might know where Landon went. And he never actually said what was discussed when he talked about his meeting with Landon at the party. We need to know what was said, or what wasn't said. It might be the key to finding out what happened that night."

CHAPTER NINETEEN

I T JUST SO HAPPENED THAT FRANK FISHER WASN'T THAT difficult to find. As Olivia and Brock were about to leave the diner, they walked past the bar and caught sight of him standing in the entranceway, talking to the manager and looking agitated. Both of them silently moved to the bar and tried to look busy as they listened to what Frank was saying at the server's podium.

"I don't want you telling anyone my business, alright?" Frank hissed. "It's not going to look good for me if you tell the cops I was seen with Landon that day. I don't want people hassling me for information."

Olivia raised an eyebrow. So Frank was worried that people were going to come looking for him. He likely didn't want to make front page news the way that Miranda had since Landon's disappearance. Olivia wasn't sure if that was enough to indicate a guilty conscience, but it was certainly interesting to her.

"Well, I don't know what you want me to say, Mr. Fisher. You're asking me to lie to the cops if they come asking?" the manager asked, folding her arms. "This is a public place. You know what you're getting into when you come here. We broadcast on our socials whenever a famous face walks in. I don't think it's any secret that you were here that day, sir."

Frank let out a sigh of frustration. "Well, at least delete the post from your socials. I just want a quiet life, alright? It was Landon who wanted to come here that day, not me. And I am *not* going to be held responsible for him going missing. I don't want anyone thinking that I had anything to do with it."

"Well then, it's a good thing you came here and started making loud demands about it, isn't it?" the waitress said coolly. "I don't tolerate disrespect in my establishment. Don't talk to me like I'm some kind of trash you passed by on the street. You're under my roof now, and being a big shot doesn't mean you can be rude."

Frank let out an exasperated sigh. "Do you know who I am, lady?" he growled. "I'll have your job for this. Of all the disrespect—"

That was their cue, Olivia supposed. Without a second to waste, they got up and swooped in before Frank could raise his voice any further.

"Is there a problem here, Mr. Fisher?" Olivia asked as she and Brock immediately badged him.

He immediately backed away and regarded Olivia and Brock with suspicion.

"No, there's—wait—hold on…"

"Hello, Frank. Special Agents Knight and Tanner with the FBI," Olivia said, but he didn't appear to be listening to her. His eyes were drifting over her body, taking her in in a way that made Olivia want to shudder.

"You? I remember you," Frank frowned. "You were at the party the other night… I didn't realize you were cops. I was going to ask for your number."

Brock was smirking as Olivia glared at Frank. "And as I recall, you were quite happy to talk about your meeting with Landon that day... so what changed? Why the sudden twitchiness? Perhaps you'd like to talk about that somewhere a little quieter."

Frank glanced around them. Some of the diners were glancing his way and whispering. He let out a huffy breath through his nose.

"Fine. I guess you've got me cornered. I'll talk... but this stays between us."

Olivia almost rolled her eyes. Frank Fisher couldn't lie low if his life depended on it, clearly. Whether intentional or not, he always seemed to be vying to be the center of attention. Olivia smiled apologetically at the manager.

"Can we head into the back room again?"

"Sure," she said with a wary glance at Frank. "But once you're done, please see him out. And consider yourself banned, Mr. Fisher."

Frank's cheeks turned red, but Olivia wasn't going to stick around and soothe his ego. She led him and Brock back to the back room and plopped herself down in the booth again, eager to interview Frank and then be done with him. She raised an eyebrow at him as he sat down opposite her and averted his gaze. He seemed to realize that he'd embarrassed himself a little.

"So, Frank. Do you feel like explaining yourself to us?" Olivia asked him. Frank ran a hand through his hair apprehensively.

"Look... I know coming in hot like that seems shady. But I didn't expect Landon to be gone this long. I thought he was just playing a little prank on us all, that he was just looking for some publicity. But the longer he's gone, the more I'm starting to think he's gone for real. And it made me realize that running my mouth at the party was a mistake. I'd had one too many margaritas. And now I'm just trying to cover my backside. The last thing I want is to be put in the spotlight."

"You mean you don't want to be put in the spotlight for the wrong reasons," Brock corrected. Frank sniffed.

"If that's how you want to put it."

"You do realize it wasn't a good look for you, the way you came in then?"

"Yes, I know. But if you want my story, then here it is. I came here with Landon that day really hoping to clear the air with him. Things have been complicated between us ever since we worked together. We fell out plenty of times, and I hate the idea of bad blood. I'm a people person; I don't like to have petty arguments making things go stale."

"And given that you slept with his ex-wife, I imagine that upped the tension somewhat?" Brock prodded, raising his eyebrow. Frank's face fell.

"How do you know about that?"

"It's our job to know everything," Olivia said plainly. "Was that something you'd planned to bring up to him?"

Frank wavered. "Yes… well, I thought about it. I wanted to see if he would bite first. If he wasn't willing to end the feud, then I wasn't about to make it worse. Not that I did anything wrong. He wronged Miranda and abandoned her. Why shouldn't I take a shot with her?"

Olivia shrugged. "I guess you're right. But it wouldn't have helped relations with Landon."

"Maybe not. But I digress. That idiot was being difficult from the moment we arrived. He chose this place with every intention of making my life more difficult, I swear. He didn't want to talk things over. He wanted to laugh in my face and have young women swooning over him for an hour of his day. So, we sat there, me trying my hardest to get him to talk, but we were interrupted every step of the way. Fans kept coming over for autographs and photos… I just sat there feeling like an idiot for even trying. I should've known that he had no intention of making things right. Landon is just a dumb drunk with nothing better to do than piss people off."

"The waitresses told us that he ordered lemonade."

"Yeah, as a chaser. He was blind drunk the whole time we were there. I think he must've had a few before we arrived, but he kept topping up his drink with a hip flask. And then he had the nerve to lie to his fans about how well his sobriety was going."

"Sounds like a frustrating conversation," Olivia said.

Frank didn't take the bait, but he did nod. "And when it became clear I wasn't going to make any progress with him nor resolve our issue, I saw no reason to stay. I wasn't about to let him drive home, so I hired a private car to take him home so that he could get ready for the show. I knew it was a big night for him… an opportunity I wouldn't want anyone to miss. I asked the driver to then wait for him to take him to the show. We all know he arrived at the event, suited, booted, and ready to go. But I don't know what happened after he left here."

"So why are you acting so shifty about it?"

"Because I was the last one to see him properly!" Frank declared. "I'm not about to get into trouble for *him,* after everything he put me through. He treated me like dirt. I gave him a leading role, an opportunity of a lifetime to star in one of my movies… and he threw it back in my face, time and time again. I hate the man. I tried not to, but I do. And that makes me look bad now that he's gone. If anyone knew that we'd been together earlier that day, had maybe overheard how the conversation went, they might not look kindly on me. I know I messed up, but I'm just trying to clear my name."

Olivia sighed, leaning back in the booth. She could see how his story added up. If what he was telling them was the truth, then they could finally account for the time Landon spent between being at the diner and heading to the event. The only thing they didn't know was who drove him, but did that matter much considering they were the one who got him safely to the event?

"You believe me, don't you?" Frank asked, a tinge of desperation in his voice. "I swear, I had nothing to do with all this."

"You might've mentioned that, Frank," Brock said impatiently. Olivia's phone buzzed in her pocket; she took it out, wondering if it might be important. When she saw what was on the screen, she sighed.

"Well, you might be in luck, Frank. It seems that the media isn't interested in you," Olivia said. Frank blinked in surprise.

"They're not?"

"No. Grayson Worth just published an article on Sebastian Morales and Miranda Morgan."

Olivia showed the screen to Brock. On it was a picture of Sebastian and Miranda dining together at an expensive establishment. They were dressed to the nines, leaning across the table to talk to one another quietly. Olivia knew it was likely they were talking about Landon, their shared connection, and the court case; but without context, the photograph looked intimate.

And Grayson Worth knew that.

"He's the worst," Brock muttered, scrolling through the article. "Why stir things up like this?"

"To entertain himself, most likely," Olivia said bitterly. "He's keeping himself relevant while all of this is going on, planting seeds of doubt into everyone's minds. He's trying to make the world believe that they're in a relationship, that they both wanted Landon out of the picture."

"Can he… can he do that?" Frank asked, his eyes shifting between Olivia and Brock frantically.

"He thinks he can do whatever the hell he wants. That's what makes him so dangerous," Brock said. "This is going to make things more difficult. We won't be able to talk to Sebastian or Miranda easily without drawing attention to the case. He's putting us on a timer before the media implodes and goes crazy."

"Why would he do that?" Frank asked.

Olivia raised an eyebrow. "Are you really that naive? You live for this kind of world, the madness of it all. He does it for the chaos, for the money, for the attention. He's fame hungry, just like everyone else in this city." She turned to Brock. "We're going to have to ramp everything up a notch. We need to check on those cars we saw in the footage and track them down."

"Yes, we do," Brock agreed. He nodded to Frank and handed him his card. "Thank you for your cooperation. If you think of anything that could help us, give us a call. And I suggest if you really want to lie low, you stop showing up unannounced at public places and causing a scene. That would definitely help."

"Um, thanks," Frank mumbled, pocketing the card. "Do you want anything to thank you for your work? I can give you an autograph, or—"

Olivia and Brock were already walking away. Olivia shook her head. Men like Frank Fisher really were ridiculous to her. And she was sure she'd have to deal with more of them before the case was over.

But time was against her now, and she needed to speed things up.

CHAPTER TWENTY

"**Y**OU KNOW HOW YOU SAID WE'D CROSS PATHS WITH Grayson Worth again?" Brock asked, looking up from his laptop. "Well, I think today's the day."

"What have you discovered?"

"The cars from the security cameras… one of them belongs to him."

"You're kidding," Olivia groaned, deflating in her seat. That was the kind of twist of fate that they really didn't need in this case. Trying to wheedle information out of a man like him wasn't easy, and he'd already proved to be a tricky customer. How were they going to find out his true motives if he wasn't willing to talk?

"Yes. That first car right next to Landon's was his. So, we have to talk to him, right? It looked like he was stalking the man or something. I know he claimed they had some kind of relationship, that they had worked together before, but I don't imagine that Landon would be happy about him following him around, fishing for gossip. Especially now that we know about his relationship with Sebastian that he was trying so hard to keep private."

"He wasn't exactly being subtle, though, parking his car right next to Landon's. No doubt Landon would recognize the car as well if this has happened before," Olivia pointed out.

"Maybe Landon knew he was there. But we can only speculate. That means we need to talk to Grayson."

"How are we going to get him to talk? Are we above bribing him?"

"I don't know. At this point, he probably knows more than we do. Way more than he should. If a bribe is what it takes, then maybe that's what we'll have to go with. But let's see if he's free to meet us and go from there. I'm not offering him anything unless we have no other choice."

Olivia found Grayson's number and dialed it, waiting for the call to go through. Grayson didn't pick up the first time, but he did shortly after Olivia tried again.

"Grayson Worth speaking?"

"This is Olivia Knight."

Olivia could practically feel the smugness radiating off Grayson through the phone. "Ahh, hello, Agent Knight. I was wondering when you would call. Are you finally catching up to me?"

"Why don't you tell me?"

"That doesn't sound like much fun. I would prefer to keep you hanging a little longer," Grayson countered.

"Well, as it happens, I'm not in the mood for fun and games. I'd like to meet with you, if you're available. We have some things we need to discuss."

"I see. Well, I don't have any plans tonight, aside from my reservation for dinner. Perhaps you'll meet me there and we can talk business. I can send you the location. And don't worry, it's nowhere fancy. I won't put you through the agony of wearing heels again."

Olivia scowled. It was as if Grayson knew everything about everything. How had he known she had found wearing heels to be such torture? She held back a sigh.

"Well, I look forward to speaking to you. I think this talk will be enlightening."

"I certainly hope so. If you want something from me, I hope you'll have something to offer in return. I would start thinking about what that might be."

Grayson hung up the call before Olivia could respond again. She let out a frustrated grunt, sliding the phone back into her pocket.

"Let me guess. He's trying to claim the upper hand," Brock said. Olivia sniffed irritably.

"Of course, he is. But don't worry about that. I have something in mind that will take him down a few notches. In the meantime, let's see about tracking down that other car."

"I already have. It's registered to a woman named Camille South. But I looked her up, and it can't be her. That woman's in her forties, and you saw the girl in the footage, right? Maybe sixteen?"

"Maybe her daughter?" Olivia mused.

"I'd have to do more digging, but I think it's likely. And she just so happened to be there at the same time as Landon... seems suspicious to me. Maybe we're looking at two stalkers and not just one."

"Maybe. But I'll bet if that's true, it didn't get past Grayson. Maybe he'll tell us more about it tonight at dinner."

Olivia and Brock spent the next few hours making notes on the case, swapping theories, and building up what they knew. By the time they were due to meet Grayson, Olivia was feeling the most confident about the case that she had since they started out.

But seeing the man again was enough to make her blood boil. He was waiting for them at the dinner table, a glass of red wine in front of him. He picked it up without a word as they sat down with him and picked up their menus.

"Whatever happened to hello?"

"I thought we could spare the pleasantries," Olivia said firmly, scanning the menu. She wasn't particularly interested in what there was to eat. She was there for business.

"Suit yourself. May I suggest ordering the spaghetti pomodoro? It's to die for. I'll be ordering it myself, by the way. I'm not trying to give you a bad recommendation. I'm not that untrustworthy."

Olivia ignored him. She felt it would be easier that way. The waiter took their orders and then Grayson took a long sip of his wine, staring Olivia down with what she supposed was meant to be an intimidating gaze. But she wasn't scared of him. He wasn't the only one with a few tricks up his sleeves.

"So. What did you want to talk about?" Grayson asked innocently. Olivia leaned forward.

"First, we'd like to know why you released that picture of Miranda and Sebastian. You and I both know that you took that photograph out of context."

"They say a picture is worth a thousand words," Grayson said with a shrug. "And I simply let my readers use their imaginations and make their own connections. I have no allegiance to either Sebastian or Miranda. I don't owe them anything. I can make their stories what I wish them to be."

"By spinning lies for the public?"

"Like I said, they came to their own conclusions about what that photograph meant. That's not my problem. It's my job to entertain, so that's what I did."

"So, now that Landon is missing you feel you can get away with manipulating stories about his life?" Brock pressed. "Even though you supposedly have a working relationship with Landon?"

"I never even mentioned Landon in the article," Grayson said coyly. "Who said this has anything to do with him?"

Olivia was running out of patience, but she wasn't about to let it show. She kept her gaze firmly on Grayson. "Well, if you're unwilling to talk about the photograph, maybe we can show you some photographs of our own." She took out her phone and showed Grayson a screenshot of his car from the footage. "Your car was parked right next to Landon's on the day he disappeared.

He was at a secret meeting with Frank Fisher, and yet you knew all about it somehow. Did you follow him?"

Grayson smirked. "No comment."

"That's fine. I figured you'd say something like that. But the problem is, Grayson, that this doesn't look good. You seem to pride yourself on nosing into people's lives where you don't belong. Landon is a very wealthy, very well-known celebrity, and you just happen to know everything about him and his life. Something that goes well beyond a typical paparazzi's job. Some people would call that stalking. The court certainly would."

Grayson's eyes darkened. "I'm not stalking him."

"That's not what it looks like to me. But please, if you have an explanation for your weird habits, please feel free to explain it to me. Otherwise, I can start looking into how the court can handle this."

Grayson looked stumped for the first time since Olivia had known him. He sipped his wine for something to do, looking away from both of them. Out of the corner of her eye, Olivia could see Brock trying not to smile.

"Fine. You've got me there," Grayson said, placing his wine back on the table. "What you need to understand is that Landon Brown and I had an... understanding. As you know, he was a very private man. He needed to be, given that his life was quickly going off the rails. A man like that wants to keep his name out of the media, and I made sure he was protected."

"For a large payout."

"Correct. Our deal was that I would keep all of his secrets. His adultery, his abuse, his... orientation. In return, he paid me a large sum each month, and I would run stories on him, but only in the way he wished me to. He paid me to show up and photograph him with other women so it looked like he was a womanizer and not holing up with Sebastian Morales. He paid me to run positive stories about him whenever he made an embarrassment of himself or needed a new PR spin. I wasn't *stalking* him. He gave me access to the GPS on his car so that I could show up unannounced wherever he might be. I've been doing him a favor, so I don't appreciate being made out to be some kind of villain. This is what he asked for."

"And now that he's missing, you're changing the narrative. Because you couldn't stand anybody having that much control over the stories you tell," Olivia said coldly. Grayson rolled his eyes, reaching for his wine again.

"Again, I'm doing my job. And I've kept my word. Nobody said I wasn't allowed to report on the state of his will. And since Landon paid me to give the public a wild goose chase, I gave them one. The farther from the truth my stories are, the safer his secrets are. Yes, people will speculate now that Miranda and Sebastian were lovers, that they were working against Landon, that they might be the reason for his disappearance. Their reputations might take a hit, but there's nothing to pin any crime on them. And in this way, I kept my word to Landon. No one will suspect the truth of the matter. I worked for Landon, not for Miranda or Sebastian, so what happens to them is not in my interest. I've kept all of their other dirty laundry hidden for the sake of Landon, so why shouldn't I finally have my fun? Besides, it's free publicity for them. They should be kissing my feet."

Olivia couldn't believe that Grayson thought he was in the right. He was in the business of ruining lives, of finding ways to drag everyone down into the depths of hell with him.

"I'm not completely satisfied," Olivia said. "If you don't want us to pursue legal action against you, then I suggest you cooperate and tell us everything else."

Grayson frowned. "What are you talking about? I've told you everything already."

"I don't think that's true. Because you weren't the only person there that day for Landon, were you? Does the name Camille South ring a bell?"

Grayson pressed his lips together in annoyance. Olivia could tell that she had hit a nerve. "Alright. I guess you're doing better than I gave you credit for. Yes, I know Camille. Well, more specifically, her daughter Hannah. And I know why she was there."

"Go on."

"Hannah runs an online fan club for Landon Brown. She claims to be his biggest fan. And she was willing to pay me a lot of money to find out where Landon would be that day."

"So again, you sold Landon out."

"I *didn't*. He agreed to it. Not to meeting Hannah specifically, but he said that he was willing to meet fans if they were that desperate. It fed his ego; he liked it. And you have to realize how desperate he was for me to keep his secrets locked down. He would do almost anything to keep me quiet."

"That must make you feel good about yourself—knowing you're so untrustworthy with information that you scared a grown man," Brock said. "And to think, all he wanted was for you to not out him to the world. That's common decency, which you don't appear to have."

Grayson was looking worn down by the conversation at this point. "Look, I'm not a monster. I would never have actually told anyone. I only had to let him believe that I might."

"That makes it miles better," Olivia said coldly. "Well, at least we know now what your involvement in this mess is. And from now on, anything you discover about this case, you come to us. Because we're not messing around. We will find a way to charge you for something. Bribery, stalking, taking advantage of a minor…"

"You can't do that."

"You're not the only one who can make empty threats," Olivia fired back, "but are they really empty when they come from FBI agents? We've got more power here than you do. So, you'd better hope that we're feeling generous, or you could wind up in prison."

"But work with us, and I'm sure we can find a way to come to… what was it you said? …an understanding," Brock added with a smile.

Grayson's face was stone cold. "Fine. You have my word."

"Good," Olivia said with a sickly smile. "And let's hope this pasta is good. If I found out you were feeding us more lies, I'm not going to be happy."

CHAPTER
TWENTY-ONE

"HOW ARE WE GOING TO HANDLE HANNAH?" BROCK asked Olivia as they left the restaurant. They'd left not a minute after finishing their meals, not arguing when Grayson said that he'd cover the bill. Olivia knew he was trying to stay on their good side, but Olivia had no intention of taking bribes from him. Once the case was over, she fully intended to report him for what he'd done, especially for taking advantage of the young woman who was Landon's superfan.

"We definitely need to talk to her. She'll need to have her parents present for this conversation, so I think now is as good a time as any. It's still early; they should all be home for us to talk to. Do you have the address registered to the car?"

"Yeah. Looks like they live out in Glendale. We can make it there tonight."

"Then let's do it. If this girl was willing to do pretty much anything to see Landon, then what else might she be capable of?"

They took a taxi to the address, and Olivia prepared herself for the conversation they were about to have. It was never easy involving a young person in a missing persons case or a murder investigation, but Olivia knew that anyone who had been tangled in Grayson Worth's web was worth talking to. She could only assume that she didn't have the full story from Grayson's side, so she wanted to see what Hannah had to say on the matter. She also knew her parents needed to know what had happened. No doubt she would get in trouble, but at least she would be less likely to do something so reckless again.

They arrived in a nice neighborhood with lawns so bright and green they could have been golf courses. They approached a white stucco house with windows so wide that Olivia could see the Souths all gathered in the living room, watching TV with their curtains open. Olivia didn't want to go in and disturb the peace, but it was a necessary evil. She and Brock thanked their driver and then headed up to the door.

They rang the bell and heard muffled talking from inside. Moments later, a young woman arrived at the door. She was wearing pajamas, and her long hair fell loose around her shoulders, making her look even younger than she was. She had a sprinkle of freckles on her nose and big brown eyes. Olivia could barely believe they had to question this girl, who she had no doubt in her mind was Hannah.

"Hannah South?"

She folded her arms around herself with the anxious look of a young adult still figuring out the world. "Yeah… who's asking?"

Olivia cringed at herself, but she had to do her job. She presented her badge. "My name is Olivia Knight. I'm with the FBI."

Hannah's eyes grew wider still. "Mom… there's someone at the door asking for me."

Moments later, another woman appeared and placed a protective hand on Hannah's shoulder. "What's going on here? It's after eight. We don't want anything you're selling."

"We're not selling anything, ma'am. We're with the FBI, and we need to ask you and your daughter some questions," Brock said firmly.

"Mom, what's going on?" Hannah asked, terror coloring the edge of her voice. "Am I in trouble?"

"What the hell are you doing, barging in here like this—" Camille started, but Olivia held a hand up to stop her.

"I promise, nobody is in trouble, ma'am. We're here to ask for help regarding an investigation."

"I understand that this feels like an invasion of your privacy, but we're here with good reason," Brock added. "We're investigating the disappearance of Landon Brown, and we need to talk to your daughter about it."

"What?" Hannah cried out, her eyes filling up with tears. "You think *I* have something to do with it?"

"The actor?" Camille asked, her forehead creasing in confusion. "Why would my daughter know anything about that?"

Olivia sighed, trying to figure out how best to word things. "We have information that your daughter dealt with a columnist named Grayson Worth. She got information from him about Landon's whereabouts, and we have security footage of her following Mr. Brown on the day he was last seen."

Camille stared at her daughter. "I thought we'd talked about this obsession of yours. He's a celebrity, and a grown man! What were you thinking?"

"Mom, I'm sorry," Hannah sobbed. "But I didn't do anything, I swear…"

"You're in so much trouble, young lady. You're grounded for the rest of the year!"

"Maybe we should have this conversation inside?" Olivia suggested quietly. Camille pursed her lips.

"Yes, alright. Come inside. Let's get this over with."

Hannah was crying softly as they all headed to the living area. Hannah's dad looked up at them as they entered.

"What's going on?"

"Dad, I'm sorry…"

He shook his head. "Were you doing something illegal on the internet again?"

"I never did that!"

"Oh, it's just something else then," Camille clipped.

Olivia and Brock stood uncomfortably while the three of them argued with one another, trying to figure out how to intervene. But then Camille clapped her hands together authoritatively, silencing the room.

"Time out," she announced a little breathlessly. "Hannah, I'm very disappointed that we have to do this. But let's not waste these people's time. They came for answers, and you're going to be honest about your answers so we can decide what course of action we need to take. Okay?"

"Okay," Hannah said meekly. Then the three of them sat down on the sofa, allowing Olivia and Brock to sit on the remaining chairs. Hannah was still sniffling quietly.

"Hannah… we need you to be very clear with us when you're answering these questions," Olivia said. "Did you pay Grayson Worth to tell you where you could find Landon Brown?"

Hannah's lip trembled. "Yes. He scammed me."

"Scammed you how?"

"He told me I'd meet my hero! He reached out to me online. I just wanted to meet Landon. I love him. Everyone thinks I'm crazy, but I love him so *so* much. And I thought maybe if I could just meet him, everything would fall into place…"

"You're delusional!" Hannah's dad snapped, but her mom shot him a warning look, and he fell quiet. Olivia looked back at Hannah.

"How much did you pay Grayson?"

Hannah's eyes were on the floor, her body trembling. "I… I can't say."

"We need to know, Hannah," Brock told her. "We can get the money back, but we need you to tell us how much you paid him."

Hannah swallowed and mumbled something under her breath.

"We didn't catch that, Hannah."

"Five thousand dollars," Hannah whispered. Olivia watched the fallout ensue as her parents gasped in horror.

"What were you *thinking?*" Hannah's dad shouted. "Goddamn it, our daughter is crazy, Camille!"

"Get out, Derek. You're only making this worse. Go upstairs, and we'll talk later."

Derek was trembling with rage as he left the room, but Olivia thought it was probably for the best that he left. He was only making Hannah clam up about the whole thing. Camille took a calming breath and placed a hand on Hannah's shoulder.

"Darling, how did you come up with that kind of money?"

"I… I took it from my college fund," Hannah said, tears dribbling down her face. She looked younger than seventeen in that moment, a child experiencing puppy love for the first time. "Mom, I love him. I'm sorry. I had to do it."

"I know it feels that way," Camille said gently. She turned to Olivia. "Is she going to be in trouble for this?"

"Nobody's in trouble. We just want her to help us with what she knows," Olivia said.

Hannah sobbed loudly. "But I don't know *anything!* I didn't even see him when I got there!"

"You didn't?"

"No! His car was there. I've seen pictures of it before, and I know it was his. But he wasn't *there.* I waited for hours and hours, but I didn't even see him… and now I've lost five thousand dollars, and my life is ruined!"

"Don't worry about the money, Hannah, we can get that back. Are you sure he wasn't there?" Brock asked.

"Why would I lie?" Hannah sobbed. "If I saw him, all my dreams would've come true. I wouldn't care what happened to me then."

"Hannah, don't say that," her mother chided.

"It's true, Mom. All I ever wanted was to see him, and now he's *gone,* maybe forever," Hannah blubbered. She collapsed into tears and sobbed so heavily Olivia thought she might be having a panic attack.

Camille looked horrified and heartbroken at her daughter's reaction. She placed an arm around her daughter and tried to calm her down, then looked apologetically back up at Olivia.

"I'm sorry about this. She's very… passionate about Landon Brown. I don't condone what she's done… but she was here the night he disappeared. She was right here with us watching the awards show on the sofa. She was shocked to find out what happened, same as everyone. I don't see how Hannah can have anything to do with this."

"I understand. I'm sorry that we had to do this, but it was important to follow every lead we have," Olivia said. "And we were hoping for an eyewitness who might be able to explain what happened that day to make Landon leave his car behind… but if Hannah says she didn't see him, then I'm sure she's telling the truth."

"I *am*," Hannah insisted through her tears. "I wish I'd seen him. I would've given *anything* to have seen him…"

"It's okay," Olivia said gently. "We believe you, Hannah. We're sorry to have caused such distress. Camille, we'll make sure the money is returned to you. And trust that Grayson Worth will also be dealt with."

Camille nodded solemnly. "Thank you. And I'm sorry about all this. Hannah's a good kid… she really is. She's just a little bit… obsessed."

"Yes," Brock said awkwardly. "We'll leave you to your evening. Hannah, if you think of anything you might have forgotten… you give us a call, okay? You want us to find Landon, don't you?"

Hannah sniffed. "Yes. Yes, please find him."

"We're trying—I promise you. And if we get him back, maybe we can tell him that you helped with our investigation. Would you like that?" Olivia asked kindly.

"You would do that? For me?"

"Sure," Brock said. "I'm sure he'd like to know the president of his fan club cared so much about bringing him back."

Hannah finally smiled through her tears. Olivia pitied the young girl. She'd been brainwashed to fall in love with a man twice her age, just because he was a Hollywood heartthrob. She'd risked herself and her lifestyle just to glimpse him. The world had truly gone mad. If only Hannah knew the person Landon really was. Maybe then she wouldn't be so infatuated.

After a quick conversation with Camille to soothe the poor woman's mind, Olivia and Brock left, both of them breathing a heavy sigh of relief to be leaving the house.

"Well, that didn't get us very far," Brock muttered. "What was Hannah possibly thinking?"

"She was thinking the same as thousands of fans all around the world," Olivia sighed. "We've put these people on a pedestal. And now they're worshiped like gods."

They called for another taxi and began the journey back to the sparkling lights of the city. Olivia's phone rang inside her pocket as they approached their hotel. She took it out and frowned when she saw who it was.

"It's Sebastian," Olivia said. She picked up the call and heard heavy breathing on the other end of the line.

"Sebastian? Is everything alright?"

"No," he whispered. "There's someone trying to get into my house."

CHAPTER TWENTY-TWO

"WE'RE ON OUR WAY," OLIVIA SAID. "YOU NEED TO call the police as well; we might not be able to make it there quick enough. Are you in a safe place? Are you armed?"

"I'm unarmed. I'm in my bedroom. I saw a figure crossing my garden. They must have managed to get through the gate somehow."

"Hold tight and call the cops. We're going to get there as fast as we can. If you can lock your bedroom door, do it. We will—"

Olivia jumped as she heard the sound of smashing glass on the other end of the line. Sebastian yelped, and the call dropped. Olivia cursed under her breath and leaned forward to talk to the driver.

"We need to change the address. And we need to get there as fast as you can. A life might be in danger."

Olivia rattled off the address as quickly as she could, and the driver obliged in speeding up. Brock's face was aghast.

"What's happening?"

"Sebastian… someone is trying to break into his house. It can't be a coincidence, right? It feels like someone who knows about him and Landon must be responsible. Why else would they target him, and only now?"

"How did they find out where he lives?" Brock wondered. "Sebastian is so private…"

"It doesn't even matter now. We just need to get there and make sure he's okay. He's going to call the cops, but I'm not sure anyone is going to reach him in time."

"He'll be alright," Brock said firmly. "We'll get there."

Olivia's heart was rushing in her chest. She felt powerless as the car sped toward their destination. At least she knew that Sebastian's house was big enough to find somewhere for him to hunker down. Whoever was attacking his home would be racing against the clock to find him.

And so were they.

"I don't think I can make it any farther than this," the driver told them. "My car won't be granted access…"

"Stay here. We'll pay you for your trouble, but we have to go," Brock said, diving out of the car. Olivia wasn't far behind him, and they took off running hard. They weren't too far from the house, but every second that passed felt like a risk. They had to get to Sebastian before the trespasser did.

Olivia couldn't understand what was happening. Was the person responsible for making Landon disappear trying to get Sebastian next? Had they already succeeded?

The gates to Sebastian's property were open when they arrived. Olivia could hear police sirens in the distance. She and Brock had managed to get there first. They raced along the dark driveway toward the house, seeing immediately the downstairs window that had been smashed. But that was fifteen minutes before. Anything could've happened in the time since, and Olivia didn't want to take any chances.

Brock went in first, leaping in through the broken window, his gun raised. Olivia followed, nodding to Brock for them to split up. As Brock thundered up the stairs, Olivia took the lower level, moving quickly but quietly through the rooms.

The house looked like it had been hit by a tornado. Papers and files were strewn all over the place, and the ornate floral arrangements that had once adorned the house had been completely trampled. The person who had broken in was clearly looking for something, but what? Some private information of Sebastian's perhaps? Something damning to Sebastian?

Or to the thief?

Olivia's footsteps couldn't be heard as she picked her way through the mess left behind. She realized she was likely following a trail to the culprit. She couldn't afford to alert them. She gripped her gun hard, ready for anything she might face.

There was rustling from the next room over. The downstairs office. Olivia took a deep breath, preparing herself. She wouldn't allow the thief to get out of there without a fight. She edged around the doorway to see a tall figure dressed in black, their face covered by a balaclava. She aimed her gun.

"Stand down," she ordered. "FBI."

The figure hesitated for a moment before running at her, barreling into her so hard that the air was knocked from her lungs. She had to fight every instinct she had not to pull the trigger as she landed hard on her back. The thief attempted to run, and Olivia wheezed as she tried to stand, the air knocked from her.

"Brock!" she cried out, but her voice was barely a rasp. She darted off after the thief, ignoring the pain and breathlessness she was experiencing.

The thief ran through the many rooms of the house, clearly a little lost in the maze. Olivia pushed herself to run just as fast, ignoring the dizzy spell that washed over her. As he headed back the way he'd come in, Olivia caught up to him, grabbing his jacket at the back. The man swung around and aimed a punch at her face, but she ducked out of the way and rammed her shoulders into his torso, winding him as he crashed against the kitchen cabinets.

She pressed her advantage and swept the man's foot; he collapsed heavily to the ground, and Olivia wasted no time cuffing his hands together.

"Don't. Try. That. Again," Olivia huffed through heavy breaths. She heard two sets of footsteps behind her and whirled around, wondering if their thief wasn't alone. But it was Brock with a terrified Sebastian in tow. Brock's face softened.

"Are you okay?" he asked, looking Olivia up and down. She nodded.

"We had a runner," Olivia grinned, breathless. "Tried to take me down."

Brock's face was a picture of fury. "I want to see his face. I want to know who dared to hurt you."

The man behind the balaclava was breathing hard, but he showed no more signs of trying to escape. Olivia yanked down the material around his face and almost gasped in shock.

"You…"

"I should've known you'd come running," hissed Grayson Worth. His eyes were a little bloodshot, and he had a crazed look about him. "Subservient little FBI agents. You're always in the right place at the right time."

"What the hell are you doing here?"

"One more story," Grayson hissed. "One more *perfect* story, and I would've been able to hightail it out of this miserable city. I wanted proof. Proof of Landon and Sebastian's little affair. I was going to tell the world, make more money than I could ever imagine, and then go. Find somewhere to retire and give this up for good. I wanted to disappear just like Landon did."

"What the hell is wrong with you?" Sebastian asked, tears in his eyes. "You scared the hell out of me… and for what? You wanted to ruin my life for money?"

"It's alright for you, sitting up in your high castle. You made more money this week than most make in a lifetime," Grayson hissed. "And your boyfriend always treated me like dirt."

"Maybe because you were blackmailing him the entire time," Sebastian snapped. "And the difference between you and me is that I don't go out trying to ruin people's reputations and lives for money. I make money because people *like* me. They like to watch my movies, and they like that I'm a good person. You could never compare. You're a monster."

"The police are coming," Brock told Grayson. He was trembling with anger, and Olivia knew it was because he had tried to hurt her and failed. "At least now we have solid charges on you. You're going to prison for a long time. You won't be terrorizing people anymore."

Grayson laughed bitterly. "You know what? Good. I'm tired of trying. I'm tired of living this life when everyone acts like I'm the scum of the earth. There are people much worse than me, you know."

"I'm sure that's true," Olivia said coldly. "I'm also sure you'll meet plenty of them in prison."

Ten minutes later, adrenaline still rushing through their veins, Olivia and Brock watched Grayson being forced into the back of a cop car. Brock put his hand on Olivia's face, checking her over.

"Are you sure you're alright?"

"I'm okay. I've got to admit, though, falling down like that rattled my bones a little."

Brock pulled her in for a hug. "I'm sorry. I should've been there to help you."

"Brock… we've been through a lot worse. Don't sweat it."

"I can't help it. I don't like the idea of anyone hurting you."

Olivia smiled as she laid her head on his shoulder and hugged him back. "I'm a tough cookie, you know. I can handle it."

"Oh, I know you can. I guess it's me that can't."

CHAPTER
TWENTY-THREE

W HEN OLIVIA WOKE UP THE FOLLOWING DAY, BROCK was already awake and scrolling on his phone. Olivia rolled over to check on him.

"Have you heard from Yara?" she asked. Brock nodded.

"She said the detox is pretty intense. I imagine when you're used to filling your body with chemicals, purging them tends to have a pretty horrible effect. She's probably going to lie low for a while, but it's for the best."

"I'm glad she's getting some help," Olivia said, squeezing Brock's arm gently. He offered her a smile.

"That's not actually what I was looking at though. Check this out."

Olivia took the phone from Brock's hands. He was scrolling through social media, where comments about Landon had gone crazy. Everyone seemed to be talking about his disappearance, wishing he would come back, mourning over him as if he were dead and gone. Olivia frowned.

"People act like they know him," Olivia muttered. "I wonder if they would feel the same way about him if they knew the things he'd done. No one likes a man who hits his wife."

"No one sane does," Brock said. "But I think he would still have a lot of love from the public if everyone found out. You'd hear a lot of 'it was only once' and 'he was drunk, he didn't mean it.' People will say and do anything to protect the celebrities they love. And look. They're even raising funds for him online. For what? Why are ordinary people paying out of their pocket to find a man who has more money than all of them combined? And where is the money even going? We're the ones carrying out the investigation. Isn't that what they're aiming to fund?"

Olivia shook her head in disbelief. "I never imagined this case would be this way. I knew there would be public opinion and people feeling the need to get involved, but this is ridiculous. These people don't know what they're doing."

"They're doing whatever they feel like they can to have some control in the situation. And someday they'll tell people that their money was what brought Landon home. Do they think he'll thank them? The world has gone mad."

Olivia continued to scroll through the social media page, shaking her head. "There are people conducting their own search parties… do they think he's just going to show up in their backyards? It's like all common sense goes out the window when people are supporting someone famous. You saw how devoted Hannah was. Imagine thousands of these people all together at once. This is going to be a problem."

"We'll just have to hope they don't get in the way. There was always going to be some craziness involved in this case. I suppose we just have to accept it." Brock took his phone back and placed it on the bedside table. "There's more. There's going to be a press conference today by the LAPD regarding the case. I think they want to get some control over the situation and remind the public that it's not their job to get involved. I think we should go. We can perhaps give a statement ourselves. It's not like we're undercover anymore. And even if we don't speak to the public, we might notice something about the people who attend. If I was the sort of person who pulled off an elaborate heist to make a famous man disappear, I think I would want to be in the room when everyone was talking about it, seeking out some of the glory for making it happen."

"You're right. Whoever did this might be lying low right now, but they might show up to something like a press conference. Especially if their handiwork is the main focus."

The press conference was starting at noon, so they dressed and headed out to meet with the police beforehand. They were greeted at the station by the officer who was running the press conference. Russell Stephenson was a tall, bald, imposing figure who had clearly been on the block for decades. He was a wizened, older man with a broad grin and shoulders that wouldn't have been out of place on a football field. He towered over even Brock, and his fists felt like ham hocks as he shook hands with them both.

"Thank you both for coming. Glad to have some assistance today," Russell told them. "I just knew we had to do something about this. It's just a mess, all over the city. Groups of people searching public parks after they're closed, trespassing, people trying to 'investigate' near the homes in the hills. Some of them genuinely think they're helping out, but mostly, they're just getting in our way and causing trouble. And the worst part is that we're spending so much time responding to calls about these troublemakers that it's turning our attention away from people in need. Huge pain in my backside."

"It's been crazy," Olivia agreed. "We've been doing our best to lie low while we've been investigating, but at this point, I think it's time we take a more hands-on approach. We're not getting anywhere with this method."

"While you give your speech, we can gauge the crowd to see any suspicious characters," Brock added. "Since we haven't had any demands from whoever did this, it's possible that they might try to use this as an opportunity to check in with the real world and see what's being said about their antics."

"Or if this is all some elaborate trick on Mr. Brown's part, perhaps he might just show up," Olivia said, rolling her eyes. She didn't fully believe that could be the case anymore, but at the same time, she wouldn't put a stunt like that beyond him. After everything she'd learned about him and the crazy world of Hollywood, her opinion of him was pretty poor.

"So, that theory goes beyond the department, huh?" Russell asked with a smile. "You're right to be suspicious. You wouldn't believe the things these Hollywood types pull. I appreciate you handling it so my team doesn't have to, to be honest. Just be aware that this event might get rowdy. There are already a ton of his fans waiting outside the hall to get in. I have a feeling it's going to be a full house."

Sure enough, as people began to spill into the building and Olivia and Brock took a seat at the front of the room, she could sense that there was unrest among the people. She'd never seen so many young women at a press conference before, and though a lot of the space was taken up by the media, every space seemed to be crammed with rabid Landon Brown fans. Olivia felt her stomach twist in discomfort. Something about the whole ordeal just wasn't sitting right with her. She was starting to wish they hadn't come.

Russell finally stepped up to his podium to talk, offering a stern look to the audience before him. He didn't seem daunted by it all, even though the room was fit to burst.

"Good afternoon, everyone, and thank you for coming. We are here today to discuss the disappearance of Landon Brown. He represents the heart of what this city is about: talent and ambition and growth. The LAPD is as devastated as anyone to hear about his disappearance. However, we would like to address the efforts of the public to assist in the case. We would like you to rest assured that we have the finest agents in the country working to find Landon Brown. Nobody has forgotten him, and though the efforts might not be visible to you as the public, we can assure you that they are very much happening. In that vein, those of you who are running your own investigations, trying your best to help out—please stop. You might not be aware of it, but you are causing more harm than good. If these actions continue, we'll have no choice but to charge you with tampering with our investigation. We know that Landon Brown is an important person to many of you. But if you would like to see Mr. Brown found, refrain from inserting yourself into a scenario that you don't fully understand. You can make yourselves most useful by staying home and keeping our communities safe."

There was a rumble of chatter from the crowd. Russell paused to allow the press to formulate their questions, but the tension in the room was rapidly rising. Olivia could see the people shifting like a wave in the crowd, bodies bustling against one another.

And then came the first cry from the crowd.

"You're not doing anything!" a male voice cried out. "It's no wonder we have to take things into our own hands! If you're working so hard to find him, then where is he? Why hasn't he been found yet?"

A cry of approval rose from the people in the crowd, and Olivia knew things were about to turn sour. She didn't know how long they had before everything descended into chaos, but she was suddenly sure that they weren't safe. The crowd was beginning to move forward, shouting over the top of one another to be heard. Olivia stood up, her heart seizing. In a crowd of that size, people could easily be overwhelmed and trampled. She was terrified that someone was going to get hurt.

"You're useless!" another voice cried out. "If Landon isn't found, it's because *you* don't know how to do your jobs!"

There was a wild cheer from the crowd. Everyone there seemed to be thinking the same, even though that couldn't possibly be true. But Olivia knew it only took a few troublemakers to start a riot. Everyone was beginning to get riled up, going along with the mood of the crowd like sheep in a pack.

"Stay calm, everyone," Russell shouted into his microphone. "Allow us to address this in a calm and safe—"

It was too late. The crowd was surging forward with voices getting louder, clamoring to be heard. Olivia saw someone go down in the crowd, and before she could stop herself, she was rushing forward to help. Brock called her name, but Olivia barely heard. There were officers flooding in from all around to hold back the crowd, and Russell was still shouting to be heard. Olivia body blocked the first few people.

"Stay back! You're going to get people hurt!" Olivia cried out, but there were already people shoving past her. Within seconds, she was packed into the crowd, unable to contain them. She yelled out, but someone's elbow caught her in the face, and she went dizzy, stumbling into someone next to her. The next thing she knew, she was shoved back, bouncing around the crowd like she was in a pinball machine. Olivia thought about everything she knew about being caught in a crowd. *Firm feet, arms out, make space.* She blinked away the pain and tried to regain her footing, but before she knew what was happening, her tailbone was hitting the ground, and she was being overwhelmed.

Panic rose in her chest. She knew she had to get back on her feet, but with bodies looming and rushing above her, she knew she'd soon end up on the ground again. Instead, she curled up tight, her arms protecting her head, and she tried to breathe as bodies pushed and shoved around her. It felt like her body was taking a beating from a thousand feet. She had to wait for the crowd to thin before she could stand.

She took her opportunity when she noticed that most of the rush seemed to have passed her. She stood quickly, turning to face the way she'd come in horror. The police were standing with shields in a row, pressing back against the surging crowd as cameramen lapped up the scene; Olivia could only imagine what the headlines would be the following day. Her legs felt like jelly, but she ran around the edge of the stampede, wanting to know that Brock was alright. More police were rushing in now, and when Olivia spotted Brock holding back the crowd, she was glad to know he was safe. This whole thing had been a disaster. How had a few rabid fans managed to mess things up so completely?

As the police got a handle on the situation, Olivia could see some of the ringleaders being handcuffed for arrest while others ran out of the hall. The surge could only have lasted a few minutes, but it had shocked Olivia's system. In a daze, she assisted the police, but in her mind, all she could think about was how lucky she was to be alive.

CHAPTER
TWENTY-FOUR

"HOLD STILL."

Olivia sank onto the hotel bed and allowed Brock to wipe the blood away from her nose. She hadn't realized until after the scrum just how badly she'd been beat up by the experience. Pain blossomed from her nose and outward, giving her the kind of headache that she knew would remain for a few days. She sighed.

"That was a mess. I never expected it to go that way."

Brock shook his head. "Most of the people who went there were practically kids. They just wanted to know what was happening to their favorite actor. But it's herd mentality... if one person starts a fight, then everyone does." Brock placed his hand under Olivia's chin and checked her over gently. "I thought I lost you. When you went down in the crowd... my first thought was just to run in and get you. And I tried, but all those bodies were pressing back against me... I couldn't move."

Olivia took Brock's hand. "I'm fine. We've been trained on how to handle these scenarios. I just hunkered down until it was safe to stand."

The worry on Brock's face didn't ease at all. "I knew you'd be fine. I knew that. But it didn't make it any easier to watch. It terrified me, Olivia. Sometimes, I wonder why we put ourselves through this. Working together."

"You don't mean that."

"I do. I don't like seeing you like this."

"You don't think having a purple nose suits me?"

The corners of Brock's lips twitched, but he didn't quite smile. "I think you'd suit anything, Olivia. But seeing you hurt is my worst nightmare."

"You forget that I know how you feel. You were in a lot worse shape after you were kidnapped. That was the worst time in my life."

"I'm not comparing. And it's not that you can't handle yourself, because you can, better than anyone. But it changes the way I think about our work. It distracts me."

"What are you trying to say, Brock? That we actually shouldn't work together? That we should be reassigned to other partners?"

Olivia was expecting Brock to wave off the comment, to laugh at how ridiculous it actually sounded out loud. But his face was solemn, and Olivia saw that he was actually serious about this. How long had he been feeling this way? They'd known all along that their jobs were dangerous—that either one of them could run into trouble at some point. They knew the risks. But Olivia knew that she would always rather be there to cover Brock's back, even if it meant suffering the stress of making sure he made it out alive. Their partnership relied on the fear they felt when they saw each other run into danger. That's what ensured they did whatever it took to get out alive.

But Olivia could understand why it made Brock uncomfortable. She felt it, too, but she pushed it aside in favor of always being there with him. But she had never seriously considered ending their partnership. How would that change things between them? How could they ever be the same when this was how they started out?

"Are we really doing this?" Olivia asked, searching Brock's eyes for an answer. But he simply looked away from her with a quiet sigh and then stood up, placing a kiss on top of her head.

"Let's get through this case first. Then we can think it over. I guess emotions are just high right now. I could've lost you today."

She rolled her eyes. "That wasn't going to happen."

Brock raised his eyebrows. "We know we can never guarantee that."

He headed into the bathroom to wash his hands, and Olivia examined herself in the bedroom mirror. She thought she looked worse than she felt. She didn't think anything was broken, and she'd been lucky to get out of the crowd with just a few bruises on her body. Was Brock right to be worried about their dynamic? However, most couples didn't have to worry about watching the other die while they were on a job together. Olivia knew that was something she could never recover from. Was it wrong of her to still want to work together anyway? She wished that Brock hadn't brought up the idea of them going their separate ways in their career.

Olivia decided that the only way she could deal with it was to push the thought away for now. *It's like he said, emotions are running high,* she thought. *He might feel differently after we finish the case.*

Olivia lay down on the bed and closed her eyes. There were things to do, but her head was pounding, and the painkillers hadn't kicked in yet. She considered whether she actually should visit the hospital, just to make sure she was okay. She could call a taxi that would arrive within—

Olivia sat bolt upright. A thought had struck her with so much force that she felt slightly wobbly after it. How had she overlooked it before? She might've found the key to the case.

"You look like you've seen a ghost. What's wrong?" Brock asked. Olivia turned to him.

"We've missed something important. Something that might fill in all the gaps in the case."

Brock frowned and sat down on the edge of the bed. "Well, what is it?"

"We have a pretty solid timeline of what happened to Landon throughout the night he disappeared... except for when he got picked up from the diner by the private car."

"But we know he made it back to his house, and then to the venue... what does that have to do with anything?"

"But here's the thing. We *don't* know he made it back to his house. We know he got in the car... and then he showed up at the show. So, what happened in that three hours? I don't think we can afford to gloss over anything at this point, considering that we don't really have any evidence to work with. And plus, we don't know anything about the person who drove Landon back and forth. You saw how crazy these fans are. We need to track them down and talk to them. Even if they're innocent, it's possible that there's something they saw or did in that time period that affected the way the rest of the evening panned out."

"I guess it's worth a shot. Should we call Frank?"

"I think we need to," Olivia said, already taking out her phone and dialing Frank's number. He picked up a few moments later.

"Hello?"

"It's Olivia Knight," Olivia said. "I need to know the name of the car service that took Landon Brown from the diner the day he disappeared."

"But why?"

"That's not your concern right now, Frank."

"Are you trying to dig up dirt on me? I have a very good lawyer; I'll call him if I have to."

"I'm just looking to speak to the company about their drivers. We're making a timeline of events. Unless you have something to hide, I suggest you provide me with their details. It's not a good look to withhold information."

Frank wavered for a moment before huffing on the other end of the line. "You're looking for Cars for the Stars. It's what most of the C-listers use to get around. I called them to pick up Landon as a bit of a dig. He wouldn't normally be seen dead using their services. But that's the only thing I'm guilty of."

"You've been a great help, Frank. Maybe have that lawyer on standby if you're so worried," Olivia said with a roll of her eyes before hanging up the phone. She searched on the internet for the company that Frank had mentioned and then called their number, closing her eyes to stave off the headache pulsing behind them.

"You're calling Cars for the Stars!" a cheery female voice greeted Olivia. It was almost like she was talking to a game show host.

"Hi. My name is Olivia Knight. I'm with the FBI."

"Wowza! We've never rented out a car to an *FBI agent* before! What service are you looking for today?"

Olivia cringed. "Actually, I'm hoping to speak to someone from your management team. We're investigating the disappearance of Landon Brown. I have reason to believe that one of your cars was hired to take him somewhere on the day he disappeared."

The silence was loud on the other end of the line for several moments. "Well, this here sounds like it might put me out of my depth!" the woman said, her cheery voice now strained. "Please hold while I put you through."

Olivia felt like she was being pranked. The whole company seemed ridiculous. It wouldn't be a shock to her if this all turned out to be an elaborate prank. She held on while bouncy music played, and she waited to be put through to management. The music cut abruptly, and someone else picked up the call.

"Hi, Agent Knight. You wished to speak with management?"

"Yes. Your company was hired by Frank Fisher last week, on the day that Landon Brown disappeared. I'm sure you've heard all about that."

"Well, yes. He called us and sent us to the Starstruck Lounge. He told us we'd be picking up Landon Brown, and we were pretty pleased with ourselves. We don't usually deal with such big stars."

"Well, I'd like to ask you some questions about that. Who did you send out to pick up Landon, and may I speak with them? I'd like to ask them about the journey they took and see if there's anything amiss."

"Well, Agent Knight, I'd love to help you, but this is the thing. Landon wasn't there when our car arrived."

Olivia's heart stopped. "I'm sorry, can you repeat that?"

"Landon wasn't at the Starstruck Lounge. Believe me—I was shocked too. Why would Mr. Fisher send us to collect somebody who wasn't there? Seemed like an awful waste of his time and money to me, but he'd already paid us ..."

"Did your driver check inside the diner?"

"Of course. Frank gave us very specific instructions to get Landon back home no matter what it took. But my driver checked everywhere. He was nowhere to be found. I figured he must've hired another car service or drove home himself. But anyway, my driver returned empty-handed."

"And you didn't think to mention this to anybody? To let Frank know that his service went unused?"

"Well, he'd already paid! And we still had to send the car out. Technically, my driver did drive that day. Just without a passenger."

"So, you're telling me that your drivers were *not* the ones who took Landon to the event?"

The voice on the other end sighed. "No, which was unfortunate. It would have been a prime advertising moment. Anyone seeing Landon Brown getting out of one of our cars would be desperate to work with us ..."

"I doubt that very much. You can't even keep track of your customers," Olivia snapped. "So, you had no interaction with Frank or Landon again?"

"I don't like your tone, young lady. No, we didn't speak to either of them that day, and we haven't heard from either since. Satisfied?"

Olivia hung up the phone. She'd heard more than enough. She looked at Brock. "I think this has to mean something important. If Landon didn't go with the car company that Frank hired, then how did he get home? According to Frank, he was wasted. He probably had no sense of where he was or where he was going. So, what happened to him in that time frame? Who took him home?"

"You're forgetting the fact that he made it to the event without any trouble. I don't see why it matters. Whatever happened to him happened at the event, not before it."

"I don't want to overlook this. Everything could be connected," Olivia insisted. "All of that time is unaccounted for. What if drunk Landon said something that got his driver riled up and that's why he was made to disappear at the event? And who knew to pick him up there in the first place? Maybe Grayson sold information to someone else that we're not aware of. If that's the case, it could've been another rabid fan who managed to drive him around without raising suspicion. And what I want to know is *why*, after all that effort to get Landon alone, would someone then drop him off at the award show before his disappearance, only to pick him right back up afterward? I don't know. There's something here—I know it. We just have to dig a little deeper."

Brock sighed. "Well, I hate to admit it, but you're nearly always right on some level. If your gut is telling you to investigate this, then we should. What's our next step?"

"I think we need to see if we can get any footage of the car. If it visited Landon's house, we might be able to get some from there. If not, then we should check out the cameras from the event. If we can get a plate on the car, then we can figure out where it came from and maybe who was driving it. That's a good place to start."

Brock checked his watch. "Is this going to be a long night?"

"You already know it is."

He smiled sheepishly. "I'll make the coffee."

CHAPTER TWENTY-FIVE

"WELL, THE FIRST THING I'M DOING IF LANDON makes it home is telling him to get some better cameras on his security system," Brock complained. "This has to be a joke, right? That we can't see the car that dropped him off on his own security cameras?"

"If it's a joke, it's not a good one," Olivia replied, rubbing at her forehead. They'd been reviewing Landon's home security videos for half an hour, only to discover that the car that dropped him off at his home was only partly visible in the footage. "But look at the way the car parked. It stopped quite abruptly. I wonder if the driver was trying not to be seen on the camera. If the driver in question is the one who orchestrated his entire disappearance, then that would make sense. The person who pulled it off wasn't spotted anywhere in the venue that we know of. They're smart. It won't be easy to track them down."

"So, what now? We already checked out the footage from the venue. We saw the car and the model type, but not the license plate. How are we going to piece that together?"

"Well, we've got the first two numbers. What if we checked online? There are pictures all over the internet of Landon's arrival on the red carpet. We might be able to find more of the license plate in the background somewhere."

He groaned. "It's going to take us all night…"

"If that's how long it takes us, then we'd better get started. I don't want this to slip through our fingers. If the person who did this knows we're on to them, then they might make a run for it. No, let's keep at it. We'll get there eventually."

"We should start with Grayson's website," Brock suggested. Olivia glared at him, and he shrugged. "He was a terrible person, but a great reporter. I'll bet if anyone has good pictures from that day, it's him. Besides, the man knew almost everything about everyone. If all else fails, I bet he knew who took Landon in their car that day. He was on the scene, after all, sitting in his car…"

"I can't imagine Grayson would help us out if we asked him. Not after we got him arrested. But you're right. His website is a good place to start."

The results from Grayson's articles weren't perfect, but they were useful. His photographer seemed to have captured Landon from almost every possible angle, revealing another letter of the license plate on the sports car that dropped him off. But more importantly, there was one photo of him getting out of the backseat of the car. In the background of the photograph, they could just about make out the side profile of the person driving the car.

"It's a woman," Olivia said. The woman had a strong jaw and sharp cheekbones, her hair cropped short and blonde. She was clearly broad and strong, even just from the small picture of her. The photo was too blurry to make out much else, but she seemed to be wearing a red outfit, and she was glancing at Landon as he got out of the car. Like she was keeping an eye on him.

"Do you recognize her? Does she seem important to you?" Olivia asked. Brock shook his head.

"I don't know… looking at her, she seems like a face you wouldn't forget, right? She's… different."

Olivia didn't like the use of that phrase, but he was right. She wasn't very feminine, and it made her stand out. Olivia could see that she was attractive, but not conventionally so. She could only see her in part, but she was sure she'd remember her face too.

"There must be a clearer picture of her," Olivia said. "There were thousands of people at the event. Hundreds of them were photographers and journalists. Surely one of them captured her face, especially when Landon was the man of the evening? Wouldn't everyone be focused on him stepping out of that car?"

But try as they might, they didn't come up with many results. Any pictures of Landon were focused on him, not the car or the woman driving it. They still didn't have the entire license plate, and they now didn't have a clear image of their suspect either. Olivia groaned in frustration, searching through yet another tabloid website.

"Maybe we're looking in the wrong place," Brock mused. "When famous stars start dating someone new, what do fans do? They create a narrative. They do background checks on the new beau and try to piece together everything about them. Imagine young female fans of Landon's seeing that there was a woman driving him around. Isn't that the kind of thing they'd notice."

"You're right. So, you think we should be checking social media?"

"Maybe? We could look into his fan accounts and see if anyone has come up with any elaborate theories about her or maybe just found a better photograph of her. Someone has to have honed in on her. If she was a man, nobody would pay any mind, but jealousy in fandoms is insane. There's no way that not a single person picked up on her presence in that car."

Olivia and Brock spent a while searching through fandom accounts, but they soon realized what a mammoth task it would be. Since Landon's disappearance, there had been millions of posts from all around the globe about him. They narrowed it down based on location tags and photo posts, but thousands upon thousands of people had tagged their location as Los Angeles to promote their posts further, and people who hadn't even attended the event were reposting the same three or four photos. Olivia rubbed at her temples, her eyes growing blurry as she scrolled through post after post. She didn't want to admit that she was getting nowhere with it.

"Wait a second," Brock said, stopping Olivia in her tracks. "That photo is one I don't recognize. Hasn't been posted much, at least."

Olivia paused to look at it. She could understand why. The photo was taken from quite far back, and it only detailed the back of Landon's body. But in the photo, there were two key points of importance. One, a clearer image of the woman's face. She was even more striking in full with her large stature and piercing eyes. But even better was the fact that the car was visible enough to make out the last few numbers of the plate that they needed.

"Bingo," Olivia said, noting down the final few numbers. Brock breathed a sigh of relief.

"*Landonlover69*, you're a real one," Brock said with a grin. "Let's run it through and see what we come up with."

When the license plate immediately matched up to a stolen car, Olivia couldn't help but break out into a grin. She knew she had been right to have a hunch about the car service. The car itself had been stolen from a five-star hotel in Beverly Hills called The Grand Piano on the day Landon had gone missing.

"This has got to be something," Olivia said, excitement rising inside her. "If we put out an APB on the car, track it down, find the driver… we might just have ourselves a suspect."

"We still don't have any evidence," Brock pointed out. "We might just have discovered that some woman decided to steal a car and take Landon Brown for a ride. It doesn't correlate yet."

"Maybe not. But I think it's going to," Olivia said firmly. "Let's go to the hotel tomorrow and liaise with them. Maybe they can enlighten us further."

CHAPTER
TWENTY-SIX

THE FOLLOWING MORNING, OLIVIA AND BROCK HEADED straight for The Grand Piano Hotel. It was a beautiful building with an interior made almost entirely of marble. There were two men stationed at the doors to turn away riffraff, and Olivia was forced to show her badge before she was allowed inside. Olivia couldn't imagine that just anyone would be allowed inside the hotel, which begged the question: How did their driver manage to steal a car from the hotel's lot without being noticed?

Olivia headed to reception and asked to speak with the hotel manager. The receptionist directed them to the manager's office where a woman who looked to be in her early forties was talking on the phone frantically. She waved Olivia and Brock into the room, but they had to sit for five minutes while she completed her call. Whoever was on the other line was squawking so loud that Olivia could hear it from where she sat, and the manager made about six dozen assurances that the hotel was fine, their clients were safe, and that they were doing all they could to ensure The Grand Piano Hotel would fulfill its responsibility to shelter and safeguard its guests. By the time she put the phone down, Olivia was filled with nervous energy, eager to move forward with the investigation and find out exactly what was going on.

"You wouldn't believe the amount of crap we've got going on right now," the woman muttered, immediately dropping her customer-service voice and speaking to them frankly. "Everyone in the damn city has something to say. Please tell me you've got that car back, or my I'll be skinned alive."

Olivia pressed her lips in a tight smile. "Unfortunately, no. We're actually with the FBI. We're here investigating the disappearance of Landon Brown."

The hotel manager dropped her head into her hands. "Wonderful. As if I don't have enough on my plate." The phone rang again, but she punched a few buttons angrily and made it go away. "Wait, why are you here then? He never was a guest here."

"We don't believe he was ever here, but we do believe that whoever made him disappear was," Brock explained. "The car that was stolen from your parking lot was the same one that posed as a taxi service in order to get him alone and later dropped him off at the show that night."

The manager sighed. "And you haven't found it yet?"

"We're getting closer, Ms… um…"

"Kendra Wilkinson," the manager replied tightly. The phone rang again, and she yanked the handset off the hook. "You can call me Kendra."

"Olivia Knight and Brock Tanner," Olivia supplied. "We're really hoping to find it soon. Who did the car belong to, may I ask?"

Kendra sighed. "It belongs to Raymond Cheung. He's an investor in The Grand Piano. As you can imagine, he wasn't impressed that his car was stolen beneath our noses, and now he's called around to every one of his high-dollar friends to completely tank our reputation."

"I know you already told the police this, but would you mind going over what happened with us?"

"It was just like any other day. Mr. Cheung came in, one of our valets took the car to park it, and it sat there untouched for hours. We have confirmed our valet wasn't responsible for the car going missing. In fact, all of our valets were accounted for when the car went missing, but someone must have stolen a uniform from the laundry room, because in the security footage, a man is seen in our red valet uniform getting into the car and driving away. So, he had to have made it past security, into our laundry room, and to the stack of car keys behind reception. The man clearly knew what he was doing."

Olivia frowned. Was it possible it was the woman they'd seen driving the car who stole it? Or was she working with someone else? Olivia leaned over to show Kendra the blurry picture of the woman.

"Does this person look familiar to you?"

Kendra frowned. "Well… if I squint, I think that might be the person we saw in the footage. My mistake, from her height I definitely assumed it was a man. But that is definitely our valet uniform she's wearing."

Olivia squinted at the photo. Kendra was right. The woman was wearing a red waistcoat over a white shirt. So, she'd likely gone straight from the hotel to go find Landon and get him into her car.

The question was still *why*? Just to have a moment in the sun with him? To get to experience his presence? But then what happened after she dropped him off? Was that it, or was she somehow involved in his disappearance too?

"So, you can't confirm the identity of this woman, I assume?" Brock asked. Kendra shook her head.

"She's not one of our employees, and I don't recognize her as a guest. We did have several deliveries here that day, so it's possible that she slipped inside then. But she must have been prepared to pull this off. I mean, you're the professionals. Do you believe she could've done that without some form of forward planning?"

"Not easily," Olivia admitted. "It does seem like she was meticulous in her plans. After all, she's managed to evade us so far, and she's barely left a trail behind her. But if you don't recognize who she is or where she came from, I think we're probably done here. Thank you for your time."

"Thank *you* for helping to track down our thief. I'll mention your hard work when I speak to Mr. Cheung. If you do happen to find the car, please, please, *please* give me a call. I've got to put out this fire before it burns the whole place down."

"Of course. You'll be first on our list," Brock said. Kendra saw them out of the office, and they headed back outside, Olivia's mind reeling.

"What are you thinking? You look like you have some cogs in motion," Brock prodded.

"I think I'm piecing it together… how she might be connected. Remember when we thought there was no way that anyone tampered with those envelopes at the event because they were in the locked room the entire time?"

"Yes… and that's still the case."

"Yes, it is. But what happened once those envelopes left the room? That five-minute window… the time period when everything went wrong. They were handed over by the ushers. Do you remember what they were wearing?"

Brock's face dawned with realization. "White shirts and red waistcoats…"

"The outfits weren't completely identical, but close enough for the woman to get away with what she did, I imagine. We saw ushers on the video feed… but what we didn't pick up on was that she was new on the scene. She must've slipped her own envelope into the stack, knowing that the first one to be read out would be her message about Landon—the message that threw everything into motion. And then, somehow, she found Landon alone and managed to smuggle him out of there… that's the part I still can't explain. The part I don't think I'll ever understand how to explain. I understand now that she must have snuck backstage by posing as an usher, and that must've been something she planned for a very long time. She knew what she was doing. I understand that she must've flown under the radar of security because she looked like she was just doing her job. And as important as the ushers were, they weren't there to be memorable, so no one questioned who was working with the envelopes and why. But then *why* did she do all of this? And how did she get Landon out of there after all this had taken place? We're running out of things to work with."

"But we have something now," Brock nodded. "We don't need those answers yet. We just need to find the woman behind all of this. I'm sure the APB will come up with something. And then we'll be laughing."

"I hope so. I don't think I've ever been so curious about why someone would do something," Olivia admitted. "I'd love to see what she has to say for herself once we track her down."

CHAPTER
TWENTY-SEVEN

IT WAS LATE AT NIGHT WHEN OLIVIA RECEIVED A CALL FROM the California Highway Patrol. She picked up the call immediately while she and Brock were working through more video footage, trying to figure out who their mystery driver was.

"Agent Olivia Knight speaking."

"Hi, Agent Knight. We've found the stolen car you were looking for. It's not in good shape. It was crashed off the 5 headed up to Bakersfield."

"And it's only been found now?"

"It's quite off the main road and pretty well concealed behind the trees. Considering the state of the car, it took a pretty big hit.

I assume the drivers were taking the road at night and that's why no one reported it. But there's no sign of a driver or a passenger."

"Okay. Can you offer me some coordinates? I'd like to come and check this out myself."

"Of course. Give me a moment. We have a crime scene team already en route."

Olivia and Brock packed up their things and headed out soon after. By the time they made it to the scene, it was close to midnight, but Olivia wasn't going to let that stop her. She fetched her flashlight out of her bag and headed over to where the crime scene team was already hard at work. A young Asian man with a friendly smile waved her over.

"You must be Agent Knight," he started. "David Song. I'm keeping things moving around here. We're still processing the scene, but there's some interesting stuff you might like to see."

"Of course. Thank you."

Olivia and Brock put on their gloves as they moved around the side of the car to look in through the passenger's window. The one on the driver's side was smashed, and most of the front of the car was crumpled inward. Whatever had happened to the driver, it seemed like they must have survived a pretty serious ordeal.

When Olivia shone her flashlight through the window, she could see that the passenger seat was covered in blood. Her stomach dropped. If Landon was the passenger, it looked like he was pretty badly hurt. Olivia wasn't even sure that a man could survive the blood loss he seemed to have sustained. Perhaps this wasn't a missing person's case anymore, but a case of manslaughter or even murder. Olivia thought of all the people who were still holding out hope that Landon was playing some kind of elaborate hoax on them all, that he was laughing at them from some private island far away. Now, as Olivia looked inside the car, she was almost certain that he was dead, or dying, somewhere in the city.

"I'm sure you're thinking the same as we are," David said solemnly as he approached Olivia. "That such significant blood loss probably resulted in death. But we've combed a hundred-yard radius. Can't find a body anywhere."

"Maybe the driver survived," Olivia offered. "The car isn't so badly damaged on that side, though it looks like the passenger's legs might have been crushed in the crash. I imagine it wasn't easy to get the bod—the victim out."

"And then how far could they get without being spotted or leaving a trail?" Brock added.

David nodded. "That's our current theory. If you look here, there are tracks leading away from the car… I know it's hard to see in the dark, but it looks like the victim's legs were dragged through the soil. There's blood here, too—a lot of it. But then the tracks quickly disappear. I'm not sure how that's possible yet, but the driver must've had some escape route. There's no sign of life in these woods, other than here. It's pretty overgrown, so it wouldn't be a very easy place to leave without leaving a trail."

"And yet somehow, they did," Olivia mused. She turned to David. "We'll call around to some local hospitals. Maybe we can figure out if anyone with significant injuries from a car crash was brought in lately, but I'm pretty sure someone would've mentioned if Landon Brown was taken into a public hospital."

"Maybe they don't have his identity," David said. "If he was in bad shape, it's entirely possible they don't have an ID match yet. "It'll be worth a try anyway."

"I'll make the calls," Brock offered. He gave Olivia and David a nod and stepped aside to do so.

"In the meantime, you can help me try to figure out where this car has been recently. If we can ping the locations via the GPS tracker inside the car, we can maybe figure out who the driver is and where they might've gone following the accident."

Olivia nodded. She was glad to be working with someone who seemed to be competent at what he was doing and ready for any possibility. She held her light steady so David could hook up his laptop to the car and work his magic.

"Looks like this car is pretty well traveled," David mused. "But that makes sense. Whoever owns it would've wanted to show it off. But whoever stole it didn't have the sense to pick a more subtle car… we're lucky that we can use this tech. Normal cars aren't quite as easy to work with."

Olivia waited and watched as he worked with the panel on the car. He let out a small huff of air.

"Okay, we're going to need to take down an address here. There are only a few locations that this car visited during the day Landon Brown went missing. First, the hotel where it was stolen from. Then, the diner where Landon was picked up for the event. Then back to his house, and then straight to the awards show."

"And from there?"

"Well, here. But there's one more location. It looks like the driver dropped Landon off at his house, but then drove somewhere in Burbank. The driver went there before picking up Landon for the evening at the show. But when the car left the show, it didn't make it back to Burbank. It ended up here."

"So, the crash happened the night he disappeared. How far is Burbank from here?"

"Not far. You can be at this house in twenty minutes if the roads are good."

Olivia's heart leapt into her throat. This was it. They were going to find their suspect.

"Alright. I'm calling in a SWAT team. It's time to end this."

CHAPTER
TWENTY-EIGHT

T HE HOUSE WAS COMING INTO VIEW. OLIVIA OFTEN thought how strange it was that the most ordinary neighborhoods could house the strangest people. The person who lived in the normal-looking house in front of her had kidnapped and possibly killed a man. She wondered how everyone around her went about their daily lives, not knowing the horrors that the woman held behind the walls of her home.

They were on the approach with a team of six other agents, with Olivia and Brock leading the way. Olivia was sure that whatever or whoever was waiting for them was nothing that eight seasoned agents couldn't handle. Still, she felt the familiar flicker of nerves in her stomach. The moment of truth was always a strange one—exciting, but terrifying at the same time.

"Do you think she'll still be here?" Brock asked Olivia as they approached the house. "Or will she have made a run for it?"

"I guess that depends on her state of mind," Olivia replied, "and whether Landon is alive or not."

Brock nodded solemnly. They were prepared for the worst. Given the state of the car crash, Olivia wouldn't be shocked if they walked in on two dead bodies. The woman might not have survived the ordeal either.

There was only one way to find out.

It was close to two o'clock in the morning. The neighborhood was asleep, and there wasn't a single sound in the air. Olivia couldn't see any lights on in the house, but that didn't mean there was no one home. Leading the way, she gestured for Brock to open the door the quickest way that he could.

He fired at the lock.

Olivia rammed her shoulder into the door to open it, and the agents spilled into the dark house. "FBI!" they barked.

She still didn't hear any sound, which she was sure was a bad sign. Either both Landon and his captor were dead, or they weren't there. She didn't believe that anyone could stay silent if they heard a shot in their home during their sleep.

It was too dark to see, and Olivia swooped her flashlight until she found a light switch. She fumbled her way into the first room she came across, finding the switch and flicking it on.

And then she wished she hadn't.

Landon Brown had been dead for quite some time. His body was propped up against a sunken sofa, and his legs were tucked under the coffee table, like he was eating at the table. Except his head was lolling to the side, and his eyes were empty.

Only now did the smell of decomposition hit Olivia's nose, making her take a step back. He didn't look quite like he did in the movies anymore, his face sunken, his skin red, and a bloody bandage wrapped around his head. Scrapes and bruises and blood covered his entire body, even dripping down to the ground in a thick puddle. It wasn't long before Olivia noticed that his legs weren't quite right either, sticking out at odd angles and almost flattened beneath his pant legs, like a 2D printout of himself.

Olivia could only assume that had come from his legs being crushed in the car crash.

"My God," Brock whispered as he came in behind Olivia.

That pretty much sums it up, Olivia thought. She'd seen plenty of dead bodies in her time, but not many quite so distorted as this one, found so late on in the process of decomposition. She found that she didn't want to look at his face, to feel like he was familiar even after his body had changed so drastically. She hadn't known him, but she'd built an idea of him in her head, seen his face a million times before they'd even met.

She hadn't wanted to meet like this, no matter what he might've done in his life.

"Secure the house," Olivia whispered to her team as they appeared to investigate what she had found. "Brock and I will take a look at the late Mr. Brown."

She could tell that the other agents were curious, but Olivia felt that the man deserved a little privacy. He wouldn't want to be seen in such a way. A man who had spent so many years crafting his public image, only to die in such a horrific way. Olivia pulled on some gloves and moved closer to the body.

The closer she got, the worse the smell became, and the worse he looked. Olivia averted her eyes to the coffee table that Landon's body was sitting at. Atop it, there was a bowl of soup that had been left untouched, and a cold cup of tea. It looked to be at least several days old, the milk congealing in the mug.

"Pretty somber tea party," Brock murmured, looking at the scene around him. "What do you make of it?"

Olivia shook her head slowly. "It's almost… loving. Like she laid out food and drink for him to take care of him. Like she was trying to make him better."

"There's no chance in hell that man survived longer than a few minutes after the crash. He would've been dead when she brought him here. And in that state… how could anyone deny that he was dead? She even put a bandage on his head. She must've known he was gone."

Maybe she was in denial," Olivia said quietly. "I don't think… I don't think this was her intention. There's no way she crashed that car on purpose, unless she was suicidal. And something tells me that she wasn't. She wanted to bring him here… for him to be brought into her life. It's no wonder she spent so long preparing for this moment. This was her chance."

"And she ruined it," Brock said quietly. "Damn… I'm no fan of Landon Brown… but this sucks."

Olivia nodded. The news of his death was going to devastate people all over the world. No matter his actions in life, he had touched a lot of people's lives through his work. Miranda and Sebastian would likely be devastated, too, even after all the three of them had been through together.

"We have to keep this between ourselves for now," Olivia said quietly. "Us and the people who need to know. We can't have everyone finding out he's dead before we catch the killer. The world will go mad."

"She's clearly made a run for it. We still don't even know her name. How are we going to find her?"

Olivia shook her head. "Let's search the house now and figure out what to do next. She's been smart this whole time, but she must've left a trail of some sort. If we find out her identity, we can make sure she doesn't leave the country. Her car's still in the driveway… my guess is that she's in a manic state and ran off without thinking. She could still be nearby, or maybe she was prepared for us coming and is hiding out somewhere."

"We can send the rest of the team out to look for her," Brock said with a decisive nod. "We're the ones who know this case best. We can search the house and look for anything that might help us make sense of this entire mess. If we're quick, we might find her by morning."

"Let's hope so," Olivia said, casting a glance at Landon's decaying body. "And then we can finally let this star die out in peace."

CHAPTER
TWENTY-NINE

❝**I**S THAT EMAIL TO WHOM I THINK IT IS?" BROCK ASKED, raising an eyebrow. Olivia sighed.

"I think it is."

The two of them were crowded around the woman's laptop, heavy-eyed as they searched for information about her. They had discovered that they were dealing with a woman named Rosemary Benton, who was just shy of thirty-five years old. And now, a quick search through her emails showed that she had been in contact with a familiar face.

"Grayson Worth has his fingers dug in every pie, doesn't he?" Brock said, shaking his head. "Looks like she's dealt with him a number of times, always paying him for sightings of Landon. So, I'm guessing she's some kind of superfan?"

"A stalker," Olivia said plainly. "Which kind of fits with everything she's been doing. And it makes sense that she always knew where to be and when. That's how she pulled off picking him up at the diner. She's clearly smart. But it seems like a lot of effort to go to. And she's spent thousands of dollars making this happen."

"You can't put a price on love," Brock said sarcastically. "It's like she'd do anything to be around him. Do you think they ever interacted? That it went beyond her seeking him out in public?"

"I don't know. I think they must have. There must've been some catalyst to make her think it was a good idea to try to steal him away. Either she thought they had some sort of connection... or he did something to hurt her, and she got mad. I'd bet on the latter. Even for someone with an obsession with another person, kidnapping is a big step. I imagine if they'd had a positive relationship, she might not be driven to do something so drastic."

"That could definitely be true."

Olivia stood up and stretched. "Keep looking through her emails. I'll take a look around the office and see what I can find."

Olivia began to look around the room. It was sparse in there, but there were nails on the wall like there used to be paintings or photographs hanging there. Olivia wondered if the room had once been some kind of shrine to Landon. If she could find evidence of that, it might help her understand Rosemary a little better.

The shelves in the room were stacked with books which Olivia had a glance through, but there wasn't much of interest there, just a bunch of trashy romance novels. *So she's a romantic,* Olivia thought. She could see how that would lead to obsession for a woman alone in her mid-thirties. She wanted somewhere to focus her energies, and Landon had been that man for her... right up until she killed him.

In the corner of the room, there were a number of cardboard boxes stacked on top of one another collecting dust. Olivia approached the top one and opened the lid, curious to see what might be inside. And when she saw, she knew she'd been right about the shrine.

Inside, there were multiple framed pictures of Landon stacked together. There were also framed newspaper clippings detailing articles about his life and his achievements. Olivia felt a little sorry for the woman. That kind of obsession had to hurt, especially if Landon didn't even know she existed. She didn't know if she was capable herself of surviving such an unforgiving existence.

Olivia lifted the box and placed it onto the floor so she could look inside the next box. Inside there were scrapbooks filled with more newspaper clippings, with photographs of Landon from magazines, and with scrawled writing about Rosemary's love for him. But as the scrapbook went on, the pictures became more personal and more disturbing. It was clear that Rosemary had taken them and printed them herself. There was a picture of Landon in the Starstruck Lounge and another of him crossing the street in New York. There were pictures that were obviously taken from places that she shouldn't have been, like hiding in bushes or behind a car.

Olivia shook her head. All this time, Rosemary had been allowed to roam around, stalking one of the most famous men on earth, building up to kidnapping and killing her idol. She'd been documenting it this whole time, and still, she had barely left a trace for them to find her. She was reckless in so many ways, and yet so good at going undetected. Was she as invisible to Landon as she had been to them?

"Brock, take a look," Olivia said, gesturing to the boxes. Brock nodded to the computer.

"We can swap. I found an interesting email."

Olivia sat down at the computer once again while Brock took a look through the boxes. She scanned the email on the screen, and then raised an eyebrow in surprise as she realized what it meant.

Congratulations, Rosemary! You have won the auction to have dinner with Landon Brown. Your bid of seventeen thousand, three hundred dollars will now be processed, and you will be meeting your idol this Friday.

You will attend dinner at Landon's favorite restaurant, Célèbre, at seven p.m. Please dress in black tie attire for the occasion, and Landon himself will greet you outside the venue. Thank you for your donation. Your money will go a long way toward helping youths in the city.

"Wow... so they actually did meet," Olivia said. "They had dinner together."

"They must have," Brock said, turning over the pages of one of Rosemary's scrapbooks in his hand. "I mean, there's no way she'd miss that, right? I think she would've skipped her mother's funeral to get a chance at sitting down with Landon. I just wonder what happened that night. Did she fall further in love with him? Did she delude herself into believing they'd be together? Or was it far from everything she dreamed?"

"What do you mean?"

"Well, why is all of her memorabilia collecting dust in the corner of the room? It's like she took it all down because she couldn't bear to look at it anymore, but she couldn't quite face getting rid of it. Maybe dinner didn't go the way she imagined it would."

Olivia pondered on that for a minute. "What if he was drunk? After all that publicity about going clean, about living a new sober lifestyle... and she meets up with him, and it's a total betrayal of the man she was so obsessed with? What if he was rude to her, made her feel bad about the way she loved him when she was nothing to him?"

"That had to hurt more than anything. Motive for murder, though? Hard to say..."

Olivia scrolled up through Rosemary's emails to the Friday of that week—the day she was due to meet Landon. There didn't appear to be anything of interest that day. But on the Saturday, there were several emails that caught Olivia's attention.

"Brock, look at this. A confirmation email saying that Rosemary had deleted her social media account. There's four of them for different sites. The user handles all mention Landon's name… she must've deleted all of her fan socials after meeting him. And why would she do that if the dinner went well?"

Brock shook his head. "He must've really humiliated her over dinner to make her give up on him as a fan. I'm guessing he made her feel pretty terrible about herself. And then the next day, she says a half-hearted goodbye to it all… takes down her photographs, deletes her socials, she just wants to be done with it."

"Until she sits with her feelings a little longer," Olivia continued. "She realizes how much of her life she dedicated to this man, and he was never going to think about her again. I bet that's how she saw it. But then what does she focus on? He was *everything* to her. He was her entire life. So, she starts to plot, to figure out a way to make him a part of her life again. To make him see her value... or to hurt him. I'm not sure which. Either way, she sets plans in motion for a confrontation. And judging by when this dinner was, over six months ago… she's been preparing for this for a long time. And she almost got away with it."

"Let's run an internet search of her," Brock said. "If she was big on social media, then maybe some other fan accounts mention her disappearing. And if we can find a good picture of her, we can run an image search on her and see if we can spot her in significant places."

Olivia typed Rosemary's name into her search engine. Sure enough, there were a number of hits for the search. There was an article declaring her to be the winner of the charity dinner with Landon. There were also a number of social media posts mentioning her, saying that she was a missed part of the fandom. In fact, it seemed that she'd been a major player in the whole thing. The accounts she'd run had once been major hubs for people to discuss their fandom of Landon. Olivia's heart sank in her chest. Did Rosemary have any life outside of worshiping Landon Brown? It didn't seem that way.

They found a clear image of Rosemary from a personal social media account. It didn't have many followers, and the photograph only received a couple of likes; but it showed her standing on a beach, awkward in her stance, wearing a bathing suit. It was easy to see here just how tall and broad she was, but she had long hair in the picture. Olivia could see such beauty in the woman, but she knew Rosemary didn't see it in herself. It was evident in the way she stood, the way her smile didn't reach her eyes. She was clearly miserable, and it was hard to look at.

"We can try the image search," Olivia said. "Run it alongside the words Landon Brown. Let's see if we can get a match."

When the search ran through, Olivia was shocked to see how many images came up. Her heart was beating hard as she examined the pictures in front of her. Wherever he was, she seemed to be. Because now that she looked closely, she could see Rosemary almost everywhere. There were more photographs of Landon in New York, where she was following close behind. There were pictures of Landon getting out of cars at events where Rosemary's face was always visible. And then there was a photograph from the scene at the press conference only the day before, and Olivia's heart stopped entirely. Rosemary had been there. The photograph showed people rushing from the building to get away from the police, and leading the charge was none other than Rosemary.

"She was in the room with us. We were *this* close to her," Olivia breathed. Brock placed a hand on her shoulder.

"She hasn't slipped away from us. Not yet."

"She must know that we're on to her though," Olivia pointed out, "because she was there when we were at the press conference. There's no way she hasn't been examining our faces, learning who her enemy is. And now that she knows there's an FBI investigation going on… she's probably running scared."

"Maybe. But maybe not. We've seen how she likes to take risks. She's shown up in places where she could easily be caught, knowing that she wouldn't be. She's been Landon's stalker for a long, long time. She knows how to fly under the radar. I think she's going to keep being bold. I mean, now that Landon's dead, I think she's got nothing else to lose."

They dug around a little more before Brock spoke up again. "Take a look at this. One of the accounts that previously mentioned Rosemary as a die-hard fan is hosting an event on Santa Monica Pier. It's to drum up some attention for the case, by the looks of things, and to rally for Landon's return. Don't you think that's the kind of place that Rosemary would want to be? With people who love Landon the way she does… or did? She alone knows what happened to him, and it must make her feel isolated. I think she'd want to be around her kind of people."

Olivia ran a hand through her hair. "I mean… it's definitely a place to start. And you're right. She's almost cocky in her approach. She might take a big risk like that. When is the event?"

Brock pointed to the screen. "It's our lucky day. The event is at noon today." "Then I suggest we try to get some shut-eye quickly. And then it looks like we're heading to Santa Monica."

CHAPTER THIRTY

S ANTA MONICA PIER WAS PACKED WITH PEOPLE WHEN Olivia and Brock arrived at eleven in the morning. It was so crowded that Olivia wondered whether they might be wasting their time. How were they supposed to find one woman in a crowd of thousands? People were bustling around, preparing for the rally, shopping along the boardwalk, and riding the Ferris Wheel. The sun was high in the sky, and tourists were already basking in the rays of the sun, even in early February.

Rosemary could be anywhere among them, and for all they knew, she might not be there at all. Olivia knew that patience was a virtue, but seeing the swarm of Landon Brown fans and hundreds of other bystanders milling around wasn't making her feel particularly confident about the whole thing.

"Don't stress," Brock said, reading her mind. "I know it might seem like an impossible task, but we know who we're looking for now. She's hard to miss."

"And yet we've missed her a hundred times before. We should've been looking for her face everywhere. It's like she's been following us too. Do you think she suspects we'll be here?"

"We can't know," Brock said, shaking his head. "We will just have to go with the flow."

"Well, we should probably become a part of the flow then. We're standing on the outside looking in. We have to become a part of it all, or we'll never spot her. If she's anywhere, she'll be right in the thick of it, right?"

"Agreed. Then let's move."

Olivia and Brock allowed themselves to get lost in the crowd. They bought coffee and stood near one another but not together. They had the rest of their SWAT team in plain clothes wandering around too. One of them was sure to spot Rosemary even if they didn't. What worried Olivia was what Rosemary might try to do if she felt cornered. Killing Landon might've been accidental, but Olivia didn't believe that Rosemary went anywhere unprepared for confrontation. She'd been sneaking around for far too long to be stupid enough to remain unarmed. She knew someday that someone would catch up to her.

And today was that day.

Twelve o'clock loomed, and the atmosphere in the air was getting more tense. Olivia could feel it in the people around her, their nervous energy, their desperation to show support and love to the man they worshiped. Olivia hated the knowledge that she had and they didn't: that Landon was gone and had been for some time. They were praying for something impossible, something that could never happen. And as soon as they caught Rosemary, the world would know that too.

The chanting began just after midday. There were several different chants going on at once, some shouting, *"Bring Landon home!"* and others declaring, *"Landon is our king."* The voices around them mingled together, creating a cacophony of noise that made Olivia's head buzz. It was hard to concentrate with so much noise, but she pretended to chant along, her eyes scanning the crowd for signs of Rosemary.

And that's when the tidal wave of people began—people shifting like the sea, trying to get out of the way of something moving fast through the crowd. Olivia strained to see what was going on. It was like someone was running through people, pushing them aside, attempting to get them out of the way.

Olivia's heart leaped into her throat as she finally glimpsed Rosemary.

There was panic on the woman's face as her head bobbed just above the rest of the crowd. She ran hard and fast, bulldozing her way through the fans around her. One of the members of the SWAT team must be chasing her. Olivia prepared herself to intercept, but just as she was about to make her move, Rosemary locked eyes with her, and realization hit her face. Pressing her lips together, Rosemary stopped in the crowd and raised her arm, holding something up to the sky.

A gun.

The shot she fired had everyone around her screaming and running like their lives depended on it. Olivia was knocked aside as several women scrambled to get to safety, but she managed to keep her footing. She had a horrible sense of déjà vu. She'd been this close to Rosemary at the press conference, too, and the chaos then made sure she hadn't even realized it. But not this time. She wasn't going to lose Rosemary again.

Olivia could see Rosemary weaving through the crowds, heading in the opposite direction as everyone else and waving her gun to clear the path. But she was heading farther down the pier, not away from it. It was perfect. Olivia knew she would come to a dead end when she met the end of the pier and the sea. She was running into a trap of her own making.

Olivia caught Brock's eye, and he nodded in understanding. They waited for some of the screaming crowd to pass before running after her, readying their guns. Rosemary had made good progress down the pier, her long legs carrying her faster than

Olivia and Brock could match, but it wouldn't matter. She'd be forced to turn around soon enough. That would be where Olivia would take her down.

They were closing in on her. The crowd was thinning, and Olivia could see vendors ducking behind their stalls to avoid Rosemary. She looked crazed as she ran, her gun pointing this way and that. Olivia's heart was hammering in her chest. They'd have to be careful. Olivia had no doubt that Rosemary was willing to fire on them. She was a desperate woman who was running out of options. She wouldn't go down without a fight.

"Rosemary, stop!" Brock called as the end of the pier came in sight. Rosemary was already slowing down, realizing her mistake as it dawned on her. She backed herself up against the railings and pointed her gun at them. Olivia and Brock came to a stop, both of them pointing their own weapons on Rosemary. Behind them, Olivia could hear the clatter of more feet catching up to them. The SWAT team had arrived too.

"Don't shoot. You're outnumbered, Rosemary. We don't want to fire on you," Olivia said as calmly as she could. Rosemary sniffed and lowered the gun but didn't come any closer to them. There was defeat in her eyes, and Olivia could see all the pain she harbored there. She was broken by it all, barely hanging on to her sanity.

"It wasn't supposed to be like this," Rosemary wept. "It was never supposed to be like this."

Everything was silent around her except from the crashing of the waves up against the pier. Olivia took a tentative step forward, and Rosemary raised her gun again, but Olivia tried not to show fear.

"I just want to talk," Olivia said softly. "I want to know what happened, Rosemary. Did you mean to kill Landon Brown?"

"No!" Rosemary cried out. "I didn't kill him! He's mine… he's always been mine. Nobody understands, but we were *meant* to be together. He just didn't *get it.*"

Olivia waited quietly for Rosemary to continue. She sniffled, tears falling from her eyes.

"I loved him for so many years. Before he even knew who I was," she whispered. "But that's unconditional love. You love without needing love back. And I did that, for so so long. I watched him marry that witch, Miranda. I watched him swan around with hundreds of other women... and I knew my time would come. It had to. I waited for so long. And then... I got my chance. I got the opportunity to have dinner with him. It was supposed to be perfect. He was supposed to fall for me the way I fell for him. I had... I had it all planned out."

"Did things... did things not go the way you hoped?" Olivia asked with as much concern as she could muster.

Rosemary shook her head slowly. She tried to speak, but nothing came out. Her body was trembling, and she looked away from Olivia.

"It felt like my life ended that day," she whispered. "At dinner he... he didn't seem to want to talk to me. He drank... a lot. He just kept drinking. And then when I told him how much he meant to me... he laughed in my face. He told me I was... pathetic. That it's no wonder I'm alone when I spend my whole life obsessing over a man that will never want me. He seemed to know exactly how I lived... he mocked me for my scrapbooks, for keeping track of his achievements, for hanging his picture on my walls... I thought... I thought I was doing a good thing. It *crushed* me. He said so many hurtful things. I knew it was the drink talking. That's what I had to tell myself. But I saw so much cruelty in his eyes. He *wanted* to hurt my feelings. He *wanted* to see me cry. And when I left, he didn't come after me. He let me go... and I let my dreams go too."

Rosemary sniffed, wiping her eyes on her sleeve. She looked younger in the moment, like a teenage girl who had just had her heart broken for the first time.

"He was my reason to be alive. And I lost it," Rosemary said, her voice crumbling. "I didn't know what to do with myself. I tried to cast him aside, to forget about him forever... but I couldn't. And then one day, maybe four months ago... I started thinking differently again. I knew he could be everything to me again. I just had to change what he meant to me." When Rosemary raised her eyes this time, her gaze was full of fury. Anger was swallowing her whole from the inside, eating away at her.

"I wouldn't let him belittle me that way again," she snarled. "I wouldn't let him cut me down to size. I decided that I would make him see my worth. I'm a *good* person. I matter. I wanted the man of my dreams to see that. And that was my intention. I was going to find him and take him home with me. I was going to show him my life and what he meant to me—just once. I would show him what he let slip away. I knew I could change his mind. I just needed the chance."

Her eyes grew darker. She gripped her gun harder, aiming it right at Olivia's head. It was like she was seeing Landon in front of her, facing her demons for the last time.

"He was resistant. He didn't understand what I needed him to do. He didn't understand that I wasn't threatening his life... I was threatening to expose how he'd treated me and make him face up to it. I was going to make him a better man—the man I knew he could be. The man he was in my mind. I loved him through it all. I loved him despite the cruelty that lived in his heart. Despite the promises he'd broken. But he didn't want to get better. He just wanted to stay the way he was. He didn't believe he needed to improve. Not the great Landon Brown, the most loved star in the world."

"So, you took him?" Olivia asked. "You wanted to punish him for what he'd done?"

Rosemary shook her head hard. "No. I just wanted to show him what life could be. I wasn't giving up. I told him as much as I drove him home. But he was so damn *stubborn*. He wouldn't let it go. And so, he grabbed the steering wheel of our car and drove us straight into the woods. Well, he certainly regretted doing that. It was hard to see my man so hurt... but I knew I could take care of him. I carried him like a baby through the night. I took him home and cared for him."

"You..." Brock started, but Olivia held up a hand to silence him. Rosemary grinned now, a smile full of sadness.

"And finally. *Finally.* He stopped fighting then. He started to understand. And he knew that it didn't matter how much he resisted anymore. He knew we were going to be together forever. He wanted to come today, to tell everyone that he was safe… but I told him that no one needs to know that. It's better if he just disappears from the world. And then it can be just the two of us."

Rosemary's eyes softened a little again, and she looked at Olivia with imploring eyes. "I promise you, you don't need to do this. Landon is safe, and he's loved, and he's happy. You don't need to break us apart. Please, I'm begging you. Let the world think he's gone. I'll take care of him like I have been since the night he went missing. I've had a hard life… a long and lonely life. Please, just let me be happy with him. We don't fight anymore, not since the crash. He apologized to me, and we're happy. So, so happy. You don't need to ruin that for us."

Olivia shook her head. Rosemary really thought he was still alive. She had deluded herself enough to believe he hadn't died in that crash. For over a week, she'd been sitting in her house with a dead man, trying to feed and clothe and care for him when he was rotting away before her eyes. Olivia knew she couldn't feed the delusion. Rosemary needed serious help, but she also couldn't be allowed to be out in society. She was a danger to herself.

"Rosemary… Landon is gone. We found him in your home. He's… he's passed away."

Rosemary blinked several times, tears forming in her eyes. "No. It's not possible. I was there just yesterday, and he was fine. He was talking to me, and holding me, and—"

"Rosemary. We need you to come with us," Olivia said firmly. "We can do this peacefully. And I promise, we will explain everything when we've got you somewhere safe."

Rosemary was trembling hard now, her knees looking like they were going to buckle. "You're lying to me! He's not dead! He can't be dead! I fixed him! I made him better!"

She waved her gun wildly, and Olivia heard her team readying themselves to shoot, but Olivia held up a hand. She didn't want them to hurt her. This woman didn't need to die. She could get the help she needed.

"Rosemary, what happened to Landon was a terrible accident. But he's at rest now. We're going to get you some help. You have to just let us…"

"No! No, no, no, no, *no!*" Rosemary screamed. The sound echoed over the ocean. "Stop lying to me!"

Despite everything she'd done, Olivia's heart broke a little for the woman. "Rosemary, please."

With an anguished wail, Rosemary fell to her knees, dropping the gun. Olivia exchanged a look with Brock, and he nodded. It was time for her to handcuff Rosemary and get everyone out of there safely. Olivia approached with caution, not wanting to spook Rosemary as she sobbed. She had broken completely now, and Olivia was sure there was no coming back from it for her.

She tried to reach out for Rosemary's wrists, but she suddenly sprang back into action, grabbing her gun and rising to her feet once more. Olivia froze in place, wondering if Rosemary would turn the weapon on her. But she watched in horror as Rosemary pressed the gun to the side of her own head, her eyes wild.

"Rosemary, no!"

The blast was loud and horrifying, rattling through Olivia's body as if the bullet had pierced her. But it was Rosemary who took the shot. It was so violent that Rosemary's body was tossed sideways. Olivia watched as her body toppled over the barriers and down into the choppy waters. Within seconds, she was swallowed up whole by the sea. Olivia closed her eyes. This wasn't how she had wanted it to end. But Rosemary's life had been a tragedy since the start. Olivia didn't think there was anything they could've done to save her.

And now, at least, she would be with Landon. Or a version of him that never existed anywhere except her own head.

CHAPTER
THIRTY-ONE

T HE HUMBLE FOREST OF BELLE GROVE WAS A WELCOME
sight after all their wandering through the Hollywood
Hills. Olivia had thought she might miss the glitz of
the city just a little, but that wasn't the feeling she got as they
drove back home from the airport. It just felt right to be back.

"I had a message from Miranda," Olivia told Brock. "She said
that she and Sebastian will be making a statement tonight. It'll be
broadcast on all major news channels."

"Why is she telling you that?"

"I don't know… I guess she thought we might like to watch?"

Brock shook his head. "Why would we want to watch that?
The case is closed. Landon is gone. What more is there to say?"

"She lost the love of her life."

"He abused her and made her life miserable."

"What's the phrase? Love hurts?"

Brock sighed. "I sympathize with her. I really do. I just don't understand why she's making a statement."

"Someone is going to have to. Sebastian isn't going to be the one, is he? He's still very much keeping his secrets to himself. And I don't blame him. He's been through enough already. He doesn't need to expose his trauma to the world."

"I guess you're right. I guess the world is waiting with bated breath. It's like this is his final movie. Except this time, he doesn't make it out alive. It's strange, isn't it … how this case almost didn't feel real."

Olivia nodded. She totally understood what he meant. Everything about it had seemed so unreal. The people they interacted with were almost like caricatures, and the places they went were locations that only the movies ever seemed to touch. Olivia thought of Yara, with the darkness in her otherwise perfect life, and Miranda, pushed aside by Hollywood in favor of the man who made her life hell. Sebastian, the heartthrob who could only love the man he wanted behind the scenes. Frank, the biggest showman of them all, scared of his own shadow in the end. These people would seem so strange anywhere outside of LA. Their problems wouldn't necessarily exist in the real world. They'd spent too long in the spotlight and become something more than human—something to be put on a pedestal they didn't necessarily need or deserve. Olivia was glad they were leaving such an artificial world behind. She knew what it meant to have a complex life, but she didn't want to lead a fake one.

Arriving home, the first thing that Olivia and Brock did was call Yara. She had returned from her spa retreat now, and she wanted to speak with them both. When she appeared on the video chat, she looked different from before. She didn't look particularly well, though her absence of makeup and glitzy clothes certainly didn't help. Her skin was a little gray, and there were bags under her eyes. But the important thing was that she was smiling. She waved to them both, and Olivia saw a glimpse of the cheery woman she had met the week before.

"Hello to you both. Are you back home now?"

"Yeah, we made it," Brock said with a welcoming smile. "Are you?"

Yara sighed. "Yeah, though I wish I wasn't. It's quiet without you two here! Makes me want to crack open a bottle of wine…"

"Yara…"

"I know, I know. I said I want to, not that I'm going to. I'm being good. I promise. The detox has left me feeling pretty rough, but that's probably normal considering this is my first time sober in a few years. Withdrawal is no joke."

"I'm really proud of you," Olivia said earnestly. "It's not easy to overcome addiction."

Yara laughed. "Well, I think I'm a long way from that yet… but guess what? I'm heading out tonight to another sober retreat! It's in the mountains somewhere, and it's pretty expensive, so I imagine it'll be good. I didn't want to sit at home with my thoughts, so I thought, why not be around like-minded people and have some fun? Although I don't recall ever having much fun sober before…"

"Yara!"

"Relax, Brock. I'm joking. I'm trying to have a sense of humor about the whole thing," Yara said with a smile. "I know I scared you, and I'm sorry. But you guys really helped me come to terms with where I'm really at. I think what I've been missing all this time is some true friends—some people willing to watch my back when I'm not at my best. I can't say I hate my life in Hollywood, because that would be a lie. But I don't really have anyone to rely on here. And I know now that I'm not on my own."

"Yara, you know I'm always here for you," Brock said.

Olivia offered a smile. "And you can count on me too. If you need us, you know where we are."

Yara's smile was practically splitting her face. "You guys… don't get me all emotional here. God knows I've cried enough tears this week. Phew! Alright, I've composed myself. Listen, I have to get going… I have a flight to catch. But is it okay if I call you from the retreat? In all honesty, I would love to hear your take on the case. So sad about Landon."

"Yes, very sad," Olivia said cautiously, but all she could think about was how he had tortured Rosemary's life and ruined Miranda's. She didn't say that though. The rest of the world wouldn't agree with her, so there was little point in saying anything. "He's at rest now."

Yara nodded solemnly. "It's good to know. I know that we're privileged people, but this world can be harsh on us sometimes too. I'm glad he doesn't have to suffer any longer. And I'll be thinking of him while I'm away. Really puts life into perspective, doesn't it?"

"I don't know about that, Yara," Brock said. "Most of us won't get kidnapped in our lifetime by our adoring fans…"

"Maybe not. But hey, you got kidnapped once, right? Can't be as uncommon as you think."

Brock spluttered out a laugh at the absurdity of their conversation. Olivia was smiling, too, despite the seriousness of the topic. Yara grinned back.

"Food for thought, right? Okay, I'll love you and leave you. See you later, alligators!"

Yara hung up the phone, and Brock shook his head, chuckling to himself. "Well, it's good to see that she's still crazy as ever… but I think I've had enough crazy for one week."

"Me too. What do you say we veg out on the sofa and get some takeout from the diner?"

Brock grinned. "You really are my dream woman. You read my mind."

"It's not hard to do. I'm pretty sure you just have the same thought circulating around your mind twenty-four seven…"

Later that night, it felt good to order in from the diner and sit in front of the TV to watch the news coverage. Brock was reluctant to give more time and energy to the people they'd met during the case, but Olivia had to admit that despite her aversion to the culture, she was curious how the celebrity crisis would be handled. Miranda had seemed like a good woman, though perhaps a damaged one. Olivia was curious what she would say about Landon. She had every right to drag his name through the dirt, to make sure that the legacy he left behind was one that people would remember for all the wrong reasons. It wasn't like he could do much about it now. But Olivia was sure that Miranda would have more grace than that.

Olivia found herself on the edge of her seat as she waited for the announcement. She caught herself and shook her head silently, disappointed in herself. She had been sucked into the whole circus, the culture she had hated all along. But still, if these people insisted on making the world their stage, then that made Olivia a part of the audience.

As the ordinary news ran on, Olivia watched the banner on the bottom of the screen reporting Landon's death. *BREAKING NEWS: FBI agents discover the shocking truth of Landon Brown's disappearance and murder.* Olivia was sure that Landon's death would be plastered all over the news for a long time. There would be no escaping it. Of all the men to celebrate in the world, Olivia knew Landon wasn't one of them, even if he'd left a mark on the world in some ways. She almost wanted to turn off the screen and forget about him, to give him no other thought. But Olivia knew Miranda wanted them to watch, and so she would.

"And now, coming in live, we have a statement about the late Landon Brown," the newscaster said solemnly. "His former wife, Miranda Morgan, will be making the statement alongside actor, Sebastian Morales."

Olivia and Brock exchanged a glance. So, he was going to be there after all. The picture on the screen cut to Miranda and Sebastian in front of several rows of press. They were both dressed in black, and Miranda was wearing a black fascinator which covered most of her face. Still, the whole world could see the red lipstick she wore, something Olivia was sure people would talk about for years to come. She was certainly making a statement that day.

"Thank you for giving me the chance to say a few words about my former husband," Miranda started. There was a distinct crack in her voice, but Olivia wasn't sure whether Miranda was putting it on or whether it was real. "Landon was many of the things that I've heard people say about him in the time since he disappeared… he was fascinating, and he was talented, and he was handsome, of course. He was one of a kind, and special in so many ways. He was unforgettable. And I know the world wishes to remember him this way."

Olivia was waiting for the *but*. Miranda paused, and Olivia held her breath, but it didn't come. Miranda took a steadying breath and continued.

"He was a hero to so many. And though he and I went our separate ways, I still loved him very much. His death has shaken the world and has cracked the hearts of those closest to him. But I fear that nobody truly knew Landon like I did. We went through a lot together, as married couples so often do. Nobody knew him the way a wife could. And today I just want to say… even your heroes have their flaws. Even your heroes can wear the mask of a villain sometimes. And that should be recognized. I have seen things in the course of the investigation into what happened to my Landon. The idolization of him made me uncomfortable. I will not speak ill of the dead… but listen to me when I tell you that Landon was not good through and through. He wasn't as perfect as you all believed... as *I* believed when I married him. And with that in mind, I would like to say that Sebastian and I will be opening our own charity to support victims of domestic abuse. It's a subject we are both familiar with… and having both experienced the tremors it can cause in people's lives, we feel it will be the best use of Landon's inheritance."

"Wow," Brock said. "I wasn't expecting that."

"Sebastian would like to say a few words…" Miranda said, stepping back from the microphone. Sebastian looked a little pale as he stepped forward, his expression grim. He looked into the camera, and Olivia almost shuddered at the pain in his gaze.

"The world has believed for some time that Landon and I were far from friends," Sebastian said quietly. "And that's true. But not in the way people believed. He was not my enemy. He was the love of my life."

Olivia sat in quiet appreciation of Sebastian as he paused. He was brave—she could give him that. He was risking a lot to speak so openly, and she admired him for speaking so truthfully.

"Few knew about the love that we shared. I always wanted it to be that way... I was scared about what people might think. But now, I wish I had shared this with the world sooner. He was my entire life. And I no longer care what people think about that." He paused, swallowing back tears. "But he did things in his life that I could never condone. I stand with Miranda as she heals from the damage that Landon did. I hope that together we can work toward a safer country for domestic abuse survivors. And as a society... I hope we can let go of putting our idols on pedestals. No one is perfect. No one is untouchable. If this whole experience has taught me anything, it's that. Be kind to one another. Be kind to yourselves. And in the absence of Landon's light in the world... let's try to overpower the darkness that remains. Let us mourn Landon, but also remember that he was flawed, sometimes cruel, and always human. Thank you for listening to me and Miranda. We appreciate your time."

With that, he turned his back on the press. They began to shout questions at him, but he simply took Miranda's hand and walked away from it all. Olivia wouldn't be surprised if they never showed their faces willingly to the world again. Olivia could see the appeal of just disappearing into the background, of making their statement their final one.

Olivia turned to Brock. "That was something."

"A moment in history, no doubt," Brock said. "And we were a part of it."

"But it won't change anything. Even after everything they've said, nothing will change."

"Yeah. No one is going to give up on their idols. No one plans to forget about the celebrities they love so much. But I'm glad they didn't sugarcoat everything that happened. Miranda deserved a chance to tell her truth. And so did Sebastian."

"I think he was brave to do that," Olivia said. "He's going to divide the world with a statement like that. People who used to love him will hate him. Those who loved Landon will likely hate him too. I guess he and Miranda will have that in common now."

"They've got each other to get them through this mess. I'm glad for that. Perhaps they can form a club with Yara for the battered and broken celebrities of Hollywood. Group therapy might do them a world of good."

Olivia gave a half smile. It felt good to put that world behind them. The past few weeks they'd experienced almost felt like a dream. And now that they were home, Olivia was happy to relish in the mundane reality of Belle Grove. Life had slowed down to a walking pace, and that was okay. Olivia had grown tired of running as fast as she could. This was what she'd been waiting for.

To her, turning off the TV and clearing away their dinner felt like walking out of a movie theater while the credits rolled. Except that the movie was long and tiring, and she was glad it was over. Hollywood had rooted itself in them, but she was happy to untangle herself from it now. They could be ordinary people once more, and normality would return to their lives soon.

And that was when Olivia heard Brock's phone ringing.

"Who is that at this time of night?" Brock grumbled, fishing for his phone. Olivia peered over to see that Yara was trying to video call him. He frowned.

"I thought she was on her flight to her retreat? Can you even make calls when you're on a plane? I guess the rules are different when you're flying on a private jet…"

"Better answer it," Olivia said gently. "She might be having a rough time. She probably just needs someone to talk to."

"Alright… but I don't want this to become a habit. I'm her friend, not her therapist. I can't be at her beck and call twenty-four seven…"

But when Brock answered the call, Olivia could immediately sense that something was wrong. There was screaming in the background of the call, and Yara's face was stricken with terror. She searched for Brock's face frantically, the screen crackling a little as if the signal was bad.

"Brock, are you there? I can't see you!"

"Yes, we're here. What the hell is going on, Yara? Are you on the plane?"

There was a delay in Yara's reply as the screen shifted and went static. But then her face returned, and she looked even more terrified than before.

"I'm on the plane," Yara confirmed. "But I think something's wrong. The plane is going down."

AUTHOR'S NOTE

Thank you for reading *Behind Closed Doors*, book 9 in the Olivia Knight FBI Series.

It's no secret that the world of Hollywood is one of glamour and allure, but there is so much more that lurks beneath the surface. This was a story we had been wanting to tell for some time, and we're so grateful for the chance to finally bring it to life. We hope that Olivia and Brock's journey through the dark underbelly of the celebrity world kept you on the edge of your seat and left you with a sense of satisfaction by the end. We wanted to create a story that was both thrilling and thought-provoking, and it's our sincere hope that we succeeded.

But we're not done yet! We have so many more exciting adventures planned for our dynamic duo, and we can't wait for you to join us on this thrilling journey. Our goal is to provide you with the perfect escape into a world of non-stop excitement and action with every book.

However, we can't do it alone! As indie writers, we don't have a big marketing budget or a massive following to help spread the word. That's where you come in! If you love the Olivia Knight series as much as we do, please take a moment to leave us a review and tell your fellow book lovers about our latest installment. With your help, we can continue to bring you more thrilling adventures with Olivia and Brock, and make our mark in the world of crime fiction.

Thank you for your continued support, and we can't wait to take you on more thrilling adventures with the Olivia Knight FBI series!

By the way, if you find any typos, have suggestions, or just simply want to reach out to us, feel free to email us at egray@ellegraybooks.com

Your writer friends,
Elle Gray & K.S. Gray

ALSO BY
ELLE GRAY

ALSO BY
ELLE GRAY | K.S. GRAY

Olivia Knight FBI Mystery Thrillers

Book One - New Girl in Town
Book Two - The Murders on Beacon Hill
Book Three - The Woman Behind the Door
Book Four - Love, Lies, and Suicide
Book Five - Murder on the Astoria
Book Six - The Locked Box
Book Seven - The Good Daughter
Book Eight - The Perfect Getaway
Book Nine - Behind Closed Doors

Storyville FBI Mystery Thrillers

Book One - The Chosen Girl
Book Two - The Murder in the Mist

A Sweetwater Falls Mystery

Book One - New Girl in the Falls
Book Two - Missing in the Falls

Made in the USA
Las Vegas, NV
25 September 2024

95783140R00125